A
Ponderance
Of
Possibilities

by Veronica Falter

To Vaughn
Enjoy

Veronica Falter

Part One

It all started with Alice. Of course, we've all heard the story of Alice in Wonderland. She had a wild adventure there, right? Well, that's not completely true. Alice was just the beginning of a much bigger adventure.

Chapter One

When the Hatter met Alice he fell madly in love. He did everything he could to make her love him back. And once he had her, he gave her fairy nectar to make her never leave. But once the courting was over and she was truly devoted he got bored. So he moved on. But he still kept Alice.

He traveled to a new realm one day on a whim. He often did that in order to find new libraries. He had read every book Wonderland had to offer (there weren't that many and when you were immortal you had a lot of time to read). He had been to many realms and read thousands of books. On this day, though, he found a book that would change the course of the fate of Wonderland.

This book was about a man with many, many wives. He had hundreds of them. Each of the wives had been wooed and had fallen deeply in love with him. When the joy of new love had worn off for him, he would lock his current wife away in a palace built especially to house the wives. Then he would go out and begin again with a new woman.

The Hatter, whose name was Alex, thought this was an ingenious idea. The man in the book wasn't immortal so eventually the wives were just there to take care of him in his old age. But for that prime part of his life, what an idea! To fall in love over and over again.

He loved Alice but he had to admit the fact that she was not immortal was a problem. She would grow old and die; even living the rest of her life in Wonderland. And with him being forever young and virile, eventually he would outgrow her. But with the idea this new book gave him, he could have eternal love.

The first thing he would have to do was build a palace. Just because he was moving on didn't mean his wife could. He was a jealous man and didn't like to share his things. Once he had claimed a woman she could never belong to another man. But with this new idea forming in his head, he would be able to keep them all. They would be kept comfortable and they would have each other for company. Alice would be the only one who would live alone for a time and she would be busy decorating the palace and getting everything ready for the others. And he would get her a pet.

He was so excited by this plan of his that he couldn't wait to get back to Wonderland and share it with Alice. He just knew she was going to love it as much as he did. After all, they had been married for five years now. Surely she had to feel the flow was wearing off just as much as he did.

He took the book home with him. He wanted her to read it so she would have a full understanding of just how brilliant his plan was. Looking back on things later, he realized that was his first mistake.

When she finished reading the book she called it chauvinistic drivel. She said it was absolutely ridiculous to think that there were women out there in any realm who would allow themselves to be used like that. He listened to her in dismay. She wasn't seeing the brilliance. Now what was he going to do? He had wanted her help designing the new castle. Maybe even with picking his next wife. But her attitude made it very clear she wasn't going to participate willingly. He was at a loss for how to proceed.

He let the subject drop for the time being. He knew that what he needed now was a way to make his women compliant. He had the nectar that would make them stay with him but that was all it did. He couldn't make them agree. He was going to have to create a new serum.

While he worked on that, though, he decided to go ahead with his plan to build the castle. He would tell Alice that this was to be a home for them and the children they would have. He felt a little guilty lying to her about that part. He could never have children. That was the price he had paid for his immortality.

He thought back on that day with a certain fondness. He had been twenty-four when he found himself in Wonderland for the first time. He had come from a poor village in a poor land. He had set out from home with a wagon full of hats his father had made. He was supposed to take them to the capital and try to sell them to nobles. As he made his way down the familiar path, though, a portal had opened in front of him. He didn't even stop to consider what could be happening. He just walked right through.

He made his way through the wilds of Wonderland until he made his way to the palace of the Queen of Hearts. She was impressed by his hats. That's what got her to start talking to him. Once he started telling her stories of what it was like in his home land, she decided to keep him as a pet.

He spent many years in her servitude. He kept her entertained while learning all of the ins and outs of Wonderland. By the time she decided to free him, he knew more about Wonderland that she did. She knew he could be a formidable enemy if he wanted to be so she made him a deal. She took his age back to what it had been when he first came to Wonderland and made him immortal. He agreed to never wage war on her and she made him rich. But she also made him sterile so that his children could never try to take Wonderland from her either.

He took his plans for the castle to Alice. He laughed to himself when she didn't even question why he wanted it so big or with so many rooms. He watched her as she imagined herself pregnant and raising their children. He knew he would have to make a forgetting serum as well as a compliance serum.

Alice took her time making the plans for the castle perfect. Alex didn't hurry her. Once the castle was finished he would move Alice into it and begin the search for his next wife. So he was willing to let her take her time because he was going to need that time to create his serums.

    Once Alice had the plans exacted to her specifications, Alex had a team of workers ready to build it. He had made some changes after she was done though. He had secret passages added that would allow him to visit different wives as he pleased. Once the palace was finished he would be able to start building the perfect life for himself.

Chapter Two

Her name was Rosemary. She had long black hair and deep brown eyes. She was working as a wench in a tavern when he first saw her. She had a beautiful smile and a low cut dress. Every man there wanted her and Alex found it thrilling that it would be such a challenge to win her heart.

His first night at the tavern he just sat back and watched. He paid close attention to the advances she paid attention to and the ones she spurned. He watched her face for indications of what she was feeling. By the end of the first night he didn't feel like he knew enough to approach her. So he went back every night just to study her.

At the end of the week he brought her flowers. She politely refused. As a paying customer she couldn't ignore him but she kept herself at a distance and was overly polite. He'd seen her do this to other men and knew this was her way of turning him down nicely. He took this as a good sign. It would be boring to win her without a fight.

The next night he brought her chocolates from Wonderland. She refused to even try them. He left them on the table when he left the tavern that night. He watched her through the looking glass on the wall as she was cleaning the tavern. He watched her find the box and open them. He watched as she tasted them. He felt delight as he saw the smile on her face. He knew he was one step closer.

He knew that after tasting the chocolate she would be waiting for him the next night. Instead of going to the tavern that night he watched her through the looking glass. He was completely delighted when he saw she was watching the door every time someone new entered. He just knew she was looking for him.

By this point he knew she would be the last one to leave the tavern. He was there and waiting for her outside the door. He had a bouquet of roses from the Queen's personal flower garden and a box of Wonderland's finest chocolate. When she saw him standing there her smile lit up her whole face.

He asked her if he could walk her home and she agreed. He stayed to the side and didn't try to touch her at all. He asked her questions about herself. She seemed thrilled to have someone so interested in what she had to say and not just her body.

He spent the next two months going back and forth between her realm and Wonderland. He brought her gifts, took her on dates, went on long walks with her, and just generally did everything he could to make her fall in love with him. By the end of that two months she was hinting at marriage.

He brought her a beautiful Wonderland diamond made from a piece of a falling star. He got down on one knee and asked her to marry him. It was a beautiful night with a pale full moon. He took her to an apple grove where the trees were in full bloom and the air smelled sweet. She had tears in her eyes as she accepted.

They spent the next couple of months planning the perfect wedding. He had kept Wonderland a secret from her. She thought they were going to live right there in the town she had lived in all her life. He wasn't going to tell her where they were going until after the wedding was over.

Alex arrived in his finest Wonderland suit. Rosemary wore a simple white dress. She had a tiara made of flowers in her hair. She had her long, dark hair in curls down her back. He thought she was a stunning vision as she walked down the aisle toward him.

The wedding was small and intimate. He brought no one from Wonderland and she didn't have much family. The ceremony was small and the reception was just a small dinner at the tavern where she worked. After the cake, he led her outside to where his carriage was waiting.

Alice had designed the carriage to look like the Cinderella carriage. It was very beautiful. It was made from a dark wood instead of the light colors Cinderella preferred but the design was the same. He heard Rosemary's intake of breath as she took in the opulence of it.

He hadn't told her how wealthy he was. She thought he was just a peddler. He had kept most of his life a secret from her. He was really enjoying watching her face as she took in the wealth he was offering her. She turned to him to ask how he afforded such a nice carriage just to drive across town.

Once they were inside the carriage he told her all about Wonderland. He told her about his manor house and the gardens that surrounded it. He delighted her with stories of the living flowers and strange creatures that lived there.

With a snap of his fingers he opened a portal for the carriage to drive through to take them to

Wonderland. He sat back and watched the wonder in her face as she took in the new surroundings. It reminded him of his first day with Alice and how the look on her face made him think that was why it was named Wonderland.

He led her on a tour through the manor. He barely saw any of their surroundings. He was too busy watching her face. Her enthusiasm was almost childlike. It was very charming. Her reactions were even better in the garden. She was delighted by the living flowers and stopped to talk to several of them.

Over the next few months she made small changes in the manor. All signs of Alice disappeared as Rosemary made the manor her home. She spent a lot of time in the garden while Alex continued his studies. The flowers reported everything back to Alex so he knew Rosemary was happy. He also learned new things about her and new ways to make her happy.

On the night of their six month anniversary he made her an amazing dinner. They ate in the garden with the living flowers singing softly to them. They had three courses; each filled with her favorite foods from home. He spent the evening telling her stories of things he had seen in other realms. He told her of fairies, elves, dragons, and even normal people. He told her of lands with and without magic.

He reveled in the happiness he could see in her eyes. At the moment he wanted nothing more than to be happy with her. For dessert he served her chocolate ice cream from the Queen's palace.

He took her to the Queen's palace the next day. The Queen wasn't there, of course. He took her on a tour of the castle and the grounds. He introduced her to some of the Queen's maids and other servants. He told her that she was welcome to visit the castle whenever she wanted a distraction from their small life. In fact, he was hoping to use her as a spy.

He hoped that her experience as a tavern wench would make her a good spy. He had an agreement with the Queen and he would never wage war against her. But that didn't stop him from wanting to know as much about her as possible. Unfortunately, Rosemary had no interest in spending time at the castle.

He didn't push the issue. He had all of eternity to learn more about the Queen. For right now he was happy just to make Rosemary love him even more.

When they reached the one year mark he took her to a ball at the Queen's palace. He had a sparkly gown made for her. He brought in a specialist to do her hair for her. He had an artist come in and paint designs on her skin where the dress didn't cover it. She was exquisitely beautiful.

It was a perfect night. The food was wonderful. The crowd was incredible to watch. They danced for hours and drank and ate too much. For Rosemary it was the most magical night of her life; even better than when she married Alex and was brought to Wonderland.

The years passed quickly after that. Rosemary aged while Alex did not. They were happy together for twenty years. Once it got to where she looked too old for him he started to grow bored with her. He went back out into other lands and began searching for a new wife. For the first time since he met her, he took Rosemary to his hidden palace and introduced her to Alice.

Thus the beginning of his harem.

Chapter Three

Mary.

Emily.

Raven.

Cindy.

Wives three, four, five, and six were all in the same pattern as Rosemary. He stalked them in the various taverns they worked in. He courted them until he won their love. He delighted them with the surprise of Wonderland.

With each wife he tried to get them to spy on the Queen and with each wife he failed. With the exception of Cindy, he stayed with each wife for about twenty years. With Cindy he got bored after about five years and sent her off to the castle before he had even started looking for a new wife. He decided that this time he was going to try a different approach with a different kind of woman.

Instead of a tavern he went to a University. In the land he had traveled to women weren't allowed to attend the University. However, at this particular one the librarian was a young, beautiful woman. He assumed this meant she would be more intelligent than his usual conquest and therefore would be harder to win.

He enrolled in the University as a student in order to have a legitimate excuse to be in the library often. He actually went to the classes and did all of the work. He enjoyed learning anything he could, so he was getting double enjoyment out of this.

His first few months on campus he went to the library nearly every day but barely spoke to her. When she wasn't paying attention he observed her but wasn't having any luck learning anything about her. All he had managed to learn was that her name was Beth and she liked the color blue. She wore something blue everyday and it wasn't because of some kind of dress code enforced by the University.

By the end of the first semester he'd barely spoken to her other than to ask where a particular book was. At the end of the second semester he still hadn't had any luck getting her to notice him. By the end of the third semester he was starting to get frustrated. At the end of the first year he was beginning to think he had picked a woman who was going to be too much of a challenge.

He went back to Wonderland for the summer and spent a lot of time watching her through the looking glass. He mentally kicked himself for having not spied on her while at the University. Then again, her personality outside of the library was like the difference between night and day.

She spent her summer outdoors. She hiked through the woods and swam in lakes. She planted flowers and talked to animals. As he watched her he thought of how delighted she would be if her plants and animals could talk back to her. He decided that that was going to be the way to win her heart. He was going to woo her with stories of Wonderland.

He knew he was going to have to go about this carefully. If he came right out and told her that Wonderland was real she would think he was crazy and that would be the end. He would have to take it little by little and hope he could lead her there.

He spent the rest of the summer writing a book about the Wonderland only he knew. He had the manuscript all set and ready to go before the semester started. Now he just had to get into her good graces enough to get her to read it. His plan was to start small and work his up to a relationship in which he could ask her if she would read the manuscript for him to see if it was worth publishing. He figured he had four more semesters before he would graduate so he had time to take it slowly.

For the first month he had small conversations with her every day. He slowly worked it up to longer conversations. Then they started having coffee dates. Six months had passed before they went out on an actual date. Even once they got to that point they continued to go slow. They only went out about once a week but as they continued to see each other the dates got longer.

It was close to the end of the third semester before he told her about his book. It turned out she was an avid fan of Lewis Carroll. She was very interested in his "take" on Wonderland. He expected her to take a while to read the manuscript since it was fairly large. He was pretty shocked when she brought it back to him at the end of the weekend.

She was fascinated by his retelling of the old story. She especially liked how he didn't paint Alice as the clueless little girl that Carroll had. Alex had written out the story the way it had actually happened. He had written out the love story between the two of them as only he could remember it (Alice had passed away some time ago). She especially loved that Alice had stayed in Wonderland to be with the Hatter. He ended the book with their 'happily ever after' and no mention of all the wives he had taken since.

She went over every part of the book with him. They spent weeks going over every bit of the book. He could feel that this project was bringing them closer than anything else could have. It made him think that maybe he had found a new pool of women to choose wives from. He pushed this thought to the back of his mind. He didn't want to jump the gun with Beth.

Once they'd gone over every part of the manuscript he asked her if she would be willing to go see the publisher with him. She agreed and they made the arrangements. The route to the "publisher" would take them through the park. Once they were out of sight of other people he snapped his fingers to open a portal.

It scared her when the portal opened. He talked fast to explain to her what was happening and hoped like hell she wouldn't run away screaming. He watched her face anxiously for her reaction. He felt relief course all through his body as her face lit up. She clapped her hands together and stepped through the portal without any further comments.

He walked at her side and watched her face as she took it all in. He always felt a sense of pride as he watched their initial reactions to Wonderland. So far they had all been delighted and intrigued.

He took her to his manor house and showed her his garden. Just as with every one of his wives, she was immediately taken in by the talking flowers. She asked him if they could stay there and never go back to the University. He convinced her to go back for the last semester so he could finish his degree. He promised her that once he had finished with that they would return to Wonderland and be married.

After the graduation ceremony she packed up the few belongings she wanted to keep and they went through the portal. They had the wedding ceremony the next day and for their honeymoon Alex took Beth on a grand tour of Wonderland. Just as he had with every previous wife he took her to the Queen's castle. Beth wasn't really spy material so he didn't even ask her to become one. Instead he showed her the Queen's library and insisted that she had free range to visit it whenever she liked. The Queen even came in to the library to meet her and agreed that she could come back as often as she liked.

While Beth was exploring the library, the Queen pulled Hatter aside. She congratulated him on finding such a scholar this time. The Queen had met each of the wives and even visited them from time to time at their palace. She was all for Hatter's marriages because it meant he was sticking to his end of their deal and not trying to take her kingdom away.

When he and Beth returned to the manor that evening she was full of stories she had heard from different people she had met in the castle. Alex learned several things that he hadn't known about the Queen before. For example, he learned that she had taken a lover from amongst her guards. She had never had a man before and Alex found this new development very interesting. He hoped it meant she would grow distracted.

Over the next few years Beth proved to be the most useful wife Alex had ever had. She became a well known and well liked figure at the Queen's castle. She often came home with information that seemed very trivial to her but was of importance to Alex. More than just being an unwitting spy, though, Alex found her to be a very useful research partner. He took her on his travels to other realms and found her insights very helpful to his studies.

For twenty years they traveled around to different realms. She helped him with his studies and gave him useful information on the Queen. When it got to the point where he would have normally sent her off to the palace and started searching for a new wife he kept her by his side. He stopped traveling and spent the next ten years at the manor house with Beth.

Together they wrote books on the different realms. They put together studies of magic that they had done. He was very much in love with Beth. He didn't fell any inclination to move on from her. He didn't even notice that she was aging. He was only interested in her mind and the contributions she was making to his studies.

Beth was in her late fifties when her mind started to go. Alex was actually depressed when he found he was losing his partner. He actually considered trying to find a cure for her but decided that in the end it wouldn't be worth it. She would still die of old age and he would stay immortal. So he moved her to the palace with the others and went back into the world to try to find a replacement.

Chapter Four

Josephine.

Hillary.

Renee.

Zoe.

Laura.

None of his next wives lasted long. He did all the same things he had with Beth but no one measured up. He kept trying though. He figured he had more than enough room in the palace for all of them so it was no big deal. Then he met Mila.

Mila was wild. She loved music and loved to dance. She loved to party. She really seemed to have no inhibitions. And the best thing about her was that she was insanely intelligent. He thought that the combination of wild and intelligent would make for a valid replacement for Beth.

He approached her at a dance one night and tried to get her attention. She danced with him a couple of times but other than that she ignored him. He didn't think much of it though because she was the same way with all men. He kept trying every night for a week with the same response from Mila.

He came back with chocolates to try to tempt her but she wouldn't touch them. He brought her jewelry and she gave it away. He brought her a beautiful jewelry box that played a beautiful lullaby and she left it on a table at the dance they were at.

Finally he decided to appeal to her intellectual side. He brought her a book. And not just any book. He brought her the book he had written for and with Beth. That she kept. The next day she found him. She threw the book at him and told him that if she wanted to read rubbish she'd go back to the University.

She stormed off and he sat there confused. He knew that she loved to read and had never seen a book she didn't like. So why was she angry?

He tracked her down the next day away from the party scene that she loved so much. She was sitting in the park. She was staring off into space and not seeing anything around her. He said her name several times with no reaction before finally touching her shoulder. She jumped and almost fell off the bench.

The look in her eyes when she turned to him made him think of the phrase "if looks could kill". Then her shoulders slumped and she turned away. She apologized to him for what she had said the day before. Then she asked him how he had learned her secret. When he just looked at her as if he didn't know what she was talking about she launched into her story.

When she was sixteen she had gone hiking in the woods. Somehow the scene around her changed and she was walking through woods that were much more beautiful than before. She saw creatures there that shouldn't be possible. Then, when the woods thinned out, she came upon a meadow with the most beautiful flowers she had ever seen. She sat down to study them and they spoke to her.

She spent hours there talking to the flowers and watching the strange creatures. She fell asleep in that meadow and when she woke up she was back in the forest she had started in. She spent years after that trying to get back to that meadow. She had almost ruined her life trying to get back. That's why she spent so much time partying now. She was trying to get her life back.

Alex nearly went hyperactive with excitement. To be the one who was going to make her dream come true and give her back her sense of self made him supremely happy. So he asked her to meet him in the park the next day for a surprise. She agreed and he went back to Wonderland for the night to see if any of the flowers remembered her.

It turned out the flowers had been responsible for her visit. Mila had been walking very close to one of the natural portals and the flowers heard her talking to the animals around her. They thought her voice was lovely and so they expanded the portal so she would walk through it. She talked with them for hours and they had wanted to keep her but knew they couldn't. So, when she fell asleep they very gently sent her back through the portal.

The flowers swore up and down that this was the only time they had ever done anything like that. Alex believed them but made them promise to never do it again. He shared Mila's story with the flowers so they could see how much that visit had hurt her.

The next day when Mila came back to the park, Alex led her a little way into the surrounding woods. He opened a portal and led her into Wonderland.

The flowers greeted her with apologies for the way they had hurt her. They believed that when she woke up she would assume it had all been a dream.

Mila was so delighted to be back among the living flowers that she wept. She sat down and started talking to them just as she had all those years ago. Over the next month Mila wandered all over Wonderland to talk to the flowers and meet the different creatures. Whenever Alex tried to talk to her about marrying him she would change the subject. After about six months he finally realized that she loved the flowers more than him and was never going to marry him.

He would never force a woman to marry him who didn't want to. However, she couldn't stay at the manor house because he was going to need to go out and find someone else to marry. He gave her a choice. If she wanted to return to her realm he would take her back but she would never be able to return to

Wonderland. If she wanted to stay, however, he would make accommodations for her in the palace of the wives. If she chose to stay she could go anywhere in Wonderland except the Queen's castle or Alex's manor house. None of his wives knew anything about the palace until he moved them there and he didn't want Mila telling any of them about it.

She agreed to his conditions to be able to stay. She couldn't bear to be separated from the flowers. Once in the palace she never wandered farther than the gardens. Thus, Mila was the first woman to move into the palace without having been a wife first.

Chapter Five

Jennifer.

Susan.

Veronica.

Nancy.

Katherine.

Anne.

Henrietta.

Joy.

Angela.

Naomi.

Delphine.

Terri.

Alex found he was growing bored with his wives quickly. He was still searching for the love he had found with Beth. He tried every kind of woman. He even courted women he never would have normally considered just in the hopes that she would be like Beth.

His current wife, Terri, was boring him to tears. He had only been with her for two years and he was certain he couldn't handle even one more minute. He made the arrangements and had her move over to the palace. She almost seemed relieved.

He went back to the realm where he had met Beth to see if he could find someone compatible. Instead of going to the University he went to the public library. A lot had changed in this realm since the last time he had been here. His first walk through the town almost made him think he would be better off going somewhere else but he went into the library first.

He felt his heart rate increase and almost thought he was going to pass out. The woman sitting at the librarian's desk looked exactly like Beth had when they first met. He knew he should turn around and walk out right then. He was setting himself up to be hurt if he pursued this woman. He couldn't help it though. He still longed for the easy relationship he had had with her. At least with this woman he could look at her face and pretend she was his Beth.

He walked by her desk and noted that her name plate read Angelica. Looking closer at her he noted that her eyes were so dark they were almost black where Beth's had been a bright blue. Also, her hair was a shade darker than Beth's had been.

He wandered through the library looking at the selection they had. He found copies of Beth's two favorite books and took them up to the librarian's desk to check out. He was hoping that they would be favorites of Angelica's as well and this would start a conversation. Instead she barely looked at him as she handed him paperwork to fill out for a library card.

He took the books and left without really talking to her at all. He went back to his manor and watched her through the looking glass. She was friendly with the regulars and with any children who came in. He watched her for a few days to see what kind of books she liked so he would have something to start a conversation with her.

He went back in to the library a few days later to return the books. He asked her if she could recommend any good books. He thought this would be less creepy than trying to start a conversation about books he knew she liked. Instead, she pulled out a pre-written list of books and handed it to him. An older gentleman standing in the stacks whispered to him that many men had tried that approach with her.

He was going to have to come up with another way to get her attention. He didn't want to try the usual stuff with the flowers, chocolates, and other gifts. He could bring her his book but he had the feeling that wouldn't work with this one. He was at a loss for what to do.

Not wanting to scare her off, he decided to take a step back. He continued to watch her through the looking glass though. He watched several men flirt with her and all of them were turned away.

He decided to stop trying to win her. He wasn't giving up. He was just going to be less obvious. So, he started reading through the list of books she had handed him. He never spoke to her about them but he knew that she noticed. It got to the point where she'd have the next one ready and waiting at her desk for him. When he had finished all the books on that list she had another one waiting along with the first book on it. He also signed up to be a children's story teller. Once a week he came in and told the children stories of other realms he had visited. The children loved his "imaginative" stories. He was simply telling them events from his life with no embellishments.

Out of the corner of his eye he could see that she was right there listening to every word. She seemed to be just as enthralled with his stories as the children were. She wasn't the only one, though. Other women had heard about him and his stories and had begun coming to the library to hear him. Now it was Angelica's turn to hear him turning down other people.

After about two years of this she finally broke down and talked to him. She asked him where he got the inspiration for the stories he told. She had always wanted to travel to other lands and explore magic. His stories had opened up that desire again. She found herself dreaming of far off places and magical adventures. She asked him if they could get together and he could share more stories with her.

He took her to a local coffee shop that evening and told her the stories that were too adult for the children. She was completely enthralled. Normally at this point he would offer to take her to Wonderland but he held back. It had taken her two years just to talk to him. If he tried to push her now she would run screaming into the night.

He let the relationship go at her speed. He let her decide how often they saw each other and what kinds of things they did. He realized that she liked to be in control so he let her take control. It took another year before she started hinting at marriage.

He watched her through the looking glass to find out what her perfect proposal would be. Then he took a month to set it all up for her. He had every detail exactly as she wanted it. She was so happy she cried when she said yes. It was a perfect imitation of Elizabeth Bennett's sister, Jane.

After the wedding he led her to the Alice carriage. Once their path led them into the woods he opened the portal to Wonderland. Then he sat back and watched her face. He was shocked when she didn't react at all. She took in their surroundings as if nothing had changed.

He pulled up to the manor house and was dismayed that she didn't look delighted. She took in the house and gardens as if they were nothing special. She didn't talk back to the flowers or the odd creatures. She didn't care at all about the furniture or decor. She didn't show any signs of interest at all until she saw the library. That was when she really came to life.

He watched as she made her way through the room taking in all the books he had collected from different realms. She was so enraptured by them that he figured he could leave the room and she would never notice. But he didn't. He sat down in his favorite chair and watched her. As he watched her he realized this marriage probably wasn't going to last. Not even married one day and he had already lost her. And to a library of all things.

He tried to make it work. For two years he tried to get her attention. It was rare for her to leave the library though. Finally he gave up and took her over to the castle. The library there was even bigger. When he told her she would be living there from then on she looked euphoric. He decided his next wife had to be someone who wasn't interested in books.

Chapter Six

Miranda.

Della.

Kaylee.

Natasha.

Holly.

Christine.

Katie.

Lauren.

Laura.

Renee.

Lorelai.

Olivia.

Anna.

Anastasia.

Bridget.

Lucille.

Arya.

Luna.

Selena.

Beth.

Brittney.

The years passed and he just kept accumulating wives. None of them kept his interest for long. None of them until he met Scarlet.

Chapter Seven

She was five years old when her mother sent her away from Wonderland. She had been so excited for the adventure. Wonderland was an amazing place to live but she was bored. Bored with the talking flowers. Bored with the musical creatures. Having been born there these things weren't oddities for her. They were just the way things were.

She would miss her mother but she never really got to spend much time with her anyway. As the Queen, her mom was too busy to really pay any attention to her. She was sending her off to learn how to be a queen from royalty in other realms. She was to spend a few years in each realm learning everything she could.

Her first stay was in a kingdom with many children. She would live with them and go to lessons with them. She was to learn etiquette and history and politics. There were no other children in the palace in

Wonderland so she was very excited to be able to spend some time with other children.

When she first arrived they were all lined up outside the castle. This castle wasn't as big as the one she grew up in but she still thought it was nice. There were five children waiting to meet her. Not one of them looked friendly or like they wanted her there.

The King and Queen of this realm seemed pleased to see her but she could see there was a forcedness to their look. She was too young to understand what was going on but she was determined to figure it out. They led her inside to show her where her room was. They gave her a tour of the castle and let her know that if she ever wanted anything the staff was there to grant her every wish.

She had been there for a couple of weeks before she found out what was happening. She overheard two of the older kids talking about her mom. It turned out the King and Queen of this realm were terrified of her mother. And on top of that her mother had threatened them with death if Scarlet was unhappy in any way.

Scarlet wanted to be liked and worried if they continued to be scared of her then she would end up being miserable. She skipped her lessons that day and went to the gardens. She was feeling lonely without flowers to talk to. She decided to practice her magic.

She was making some twigs dance around when the other children came across her. For the first time since she had arrived at the castle they were looking at her with genuine interest. They had never seen magic before. They spent the rest of the day delighted as she did different tricks.

After that the family actually took the time to get to know her and accepted her for her. She was incredibly intelligent. She excelled in her lessons. But she was also incredibly sweet. She was nice to everyone in such a sincere way that soon everyone in the castle held her in the highest regard.

She expected her mother to check in on her but other than the occasional letter she stayed away. At first this made Scarlet sad. But after a couple of years of study she realized that as Queen her mother had a lot on her plate. And she had arranged for her to be taught by powerful rulers. Scarlet knew that Wonderland meant a great deal to her mother and that it was very important to her that Scarlet be the type of leader Wonderland needed.

See, the Queen hadn't been born in Wonderland. She had been the Princess of a small realm. There was no magic in that realm yet she, Regina, had been born with magic. This was kept hidden, though, because the people of the realm were superstitious people.

One day a strange traveler came to the realm. He was a very young man and very handsome. He got a job at the castle working in the stables. He wasn't there for a love of horses, though. He was learning everything he could about the royal family. He wanted to marry the Princess and believed if he could find a big enough secret he would have a way to blackmail them into giving him her hand.

He followed Regina into the woods one day and saw her doing magic. He knew he had his bargaining chip. Her parents would have to let him marry her if they wanted to protect their secret. He went to the King and Queen and demanded that they marry Regina to him. They had no choice but to agree.

When they told Regina she refused to marry him. She didn't care that he was handsome or young. She refused to marry someone who was only after her for her position and not for love. She confronted him and he told her she was nothing but a stupid woman and she would have to do what she was told.

She slapped him hard across the face and then ran off. He chased after her. She was terrified and had no idea where she was going. She just ran blindly. In her panic her magic started crackling out of her hands. A portal opened up in front of her and she ran through it.

She was running fast but he was faster. He made it through the portal behind her before it closed. She kept running, completely unaware of the changes in the environment around her. She was sure he was going to catch her any second but then she heard a strangled cry from behind her. She turned back to see that he was being held in place by two large trees.

She stopped and stared. For the first time she took in her surroundings and realized that she was not in her beloved forest. She turned in a slow circle to see if there was anyone else around; someone who had controlled the trees and saved her. She saw no people but there were odd little creatures all around and it seemed as if the flowers were whispering.

Finally the trees spoke to her. They told her that they could feel the magic coming from her. There was a prophecy from long ago that a stranger from another land would come to rule them and they would know this new ruler by her magic. No one batted an eye at magic in Wonderland.

The trees snapped the neck of her pursuer and buried him in the dirt. She was shocked at the swiftness of it. The trees told her they wanted her to feel safe so that she would stay. She looked at their open and honest faces and listened to the flowers begging her to stay. She thought of spending her whole life having to hide her magic. She thought about her parents trying to force her into marriage to keep her secret. She looked again at the trees, creatures, and flowers and made the decision to stay.

Regina spent years building up Wonderland into a realm that all others wanted to be in. But she was also ruthless. She was never going to let others control her life again. She wanted Scarlet to continue on when she was ready to step down but she wanted Scarlet to rule her own way. That was why she sent her out to learn from other realms.

Scarlet was ten when she left the first realm. She was sad to leave. She had grown to love this family. But she understood the need and was looking forward to learning all she could in order to be a good ruler.

Chapter Eight

At the age of ten she entered her second realm. There were only two kids in this realm. Her previous guardians had sent word ahead of her about what a great kid she was. She was greeted with open arms and curiosity rather than hostility this time.

In the first realm she had learned the importance of getting others to like her so that things would go smoothly. She used her magic to manipulate the kids into stopping their hostilities. She didn't use it on them. She just used it to do tricks that kept them entertained.

With the commendation from her first family she didn't think she would need her magic again. She fell into a routine of studies and playing. She got along well with the children. But she was more interested in studying the King and Queen. She observed them every chance she got.

Even at the age of ten she could tell they were weak. They were easily manipulated by their advisor. She watched the advisor as well but couldn't find anything at all special about him. He just really liked power and the King and Queen were too weak willed to stand against him.

In this realm she learned how to be stealthy. She snuck around the castle and learned every place there was to hide. She learned every secret there was to know about everyone who lived there. From the highest up, the King and Queen, to the lowest servant, the stable boy, she knew it all.

She decided in her last year there to use this knowledge to her advantage. She picked her favorite of the two children and started training her. She showed her the hiding spaces. She taught her all the secrets. She set her up to take on the advisor and take over the kingdom. She knew in doing all of this she was creating an ally.

The year seemed to fly by. She learned a lot from teaching her new ally how to take over. Her last week in the realm she and her ally put all their plans in place. They devised a way to stay in touch when she went on to her next realm. The ally, Sharon, was going to pass all new information on to her. Scarlet was then going to come back in two years when Sharon turned eighteen and help her take over.

Scarlet had a new plan in place for herself. She had really enjoyed learning secrets and planning the coup. She decided she was going to do this in every realm. She would learn all the secrets and then hand-pick the new leader. This way she was leaving a string of strong allies that she would be able to call on later if she needed them.

Chapter Nine

She was thirteen when she left the second realm. Sharon gave her some helpful hints on how to train the next ally. She was very excited to start her next project. This new realm had seven children for her to choose from. She just hoped one of them would live up to her hopes.

The King in this realm was a single father. His wife had died giving birth to the youngest child a few years before. He was lonely and depressed and paid very little attention to anything happening in the kingdom.

It didn't take Scarlet long to find all the ways to hide in the castle and learn people's secrets. She realized very quickly that the oldest son, a fifteen-year-old boy named Anthony, was actually running everything. He was actually very good at it. He was compassionate and fair. He took everything seriously and was swift with his justice. Once he set a sentence he carried it out immediately.

She thought he would make an excellent ally without her even having to train him. She sent messages back and forth with Sharon and she agreed with Scarlet's assessment. All that was left for her to do was find a way to approach him.

She knew from the way he talked to her that he thought she was a little kid. That irritated the crap out of her. She knew more about politics than he did. And she had magic. Then it struck her.....he didn't know about her magic.

She convinced her tutor to have Anthony come to one of her classes. The pretense was that he was to walk her through some of the policies in place that he followed. Once he was there she was going to show him her magic. She knew that wouldn't be enough but she hoped it would get his attention. Once she had his attention she could bring him into her circle.

The lesson went much better than she thought it would. He really knew the policies of his country and was an excellent teacher. She learned a lot from just the one talk with him. Instead of showing him her magic she asked him if they could have more private lessons. He agreed and thus began the beginning of an amazing friendship.

She was passing a lot of what she learned on to Sharon. Sharon was putting the information to good use. She had managed to replace the advisor without him even realizing it. He couldn't understand why the King and Queen were changing policies despite what he was telling them to do.

About six months after they started their lessons, Scarlet discovered a big secret about Anthony. She came across him late one night in a deserted part of the castle. He had a handful of twigs and he was making them dance. It reminded her of how she won over the family in her first realm.

She stood in the doorway and watched him. When he noticed her he jumped about a foot in the air and began to stutter and stammer. She let out a little giggle. She stepped into the room and closed the door behind her. Then, with a flick of her wrist, she set the twigs to dancing around the room. He stared at her in shock and awe.

She burst into laughter. Once she stopped laughing and could breath normally again, she started his first lesson. For the next couple of hours she worked with him on the basics. By the time they gave in and went to bed for the night he was getting really good with his magic.

For the next month she observed him during the day with his subjects then continued politics lessons in the afternoons. Then, when the rest of the castle was asleep, they worked on his magic. He mastered things quickly. Even Sharon was impressed with him when she read the reports Scarlet sent her.

When it was getting closer to Sharon's eighteenth birthday and the time they had planned for her to take over her kingdom, Scarlet told Anthony about it. He had some suggestions about a few ways to make it go smoother. In the end he decided to go with Scarlet and help them oust the advisor.

All three of them were surprised with how easy it was. Sharon had been doing so well at controlling her parents that the advisor had already been feeling ousted. He went away peacefully. What was even more of a surprise to them was the instant chemistry between Sharon and Anthony. Scarlet was certain there would be a union between the two realms within five years.

When Scarlet and Anthony went back to his realm, she taught him her and Sharon's way of communicating so that they could grow their budding romance. He was pleasantly surprised to learn it was nothing more than enchanted mirrors.

It wasn't long after that that it was time for Scarlet to move on. She was fifteen at this point. She was a little sad about leaving this realm. She really loved her lessons with Anthony. She was a little trepidatious about moving on this time. She was older now and thought it might be harder to continue.

She knew she had to though. She was too young to return and try to rule. Plus she was determined to continue to build allies. So she moved on.

Chapter Ten

Fifteen and another new realm. She had no plan in place this time. She was going to do her spying and see if that led her anywhere. If she had learned anything from the last realm it was that people could surprise you. She knew that so far she had been lucky in finding allies. There may not be anyone in this realm who would want to work with her.

In this realm there was a Queen with no King. There were ten children here and each one had a different father. The Queen didn't believe in love or marriage. She did believe in children though. The problem was that she wanted to train her children to take over other realms rather than rule the one they had.

Scarlet went through the studies and listened as the kids were taught how to take over realms. Scarlet kept any comments she had to herself. She didn't want to rock the boat. However, whenever she wasn't at lessons or expected to be somewhere else she was sneaking through the castle to learn anything she could.

After only a few weeks she found a hidden passage that went behind the Queen's chamber. She stood and listened as the Queen made plans with her oldest child. She was making plans for him to use Scarlet as a bargaining chip. He was to use her as a hostage in order to force Regina to marry him. Once the wedding had taken place he would lock Regina away and take Wonderland for himself.

Scarlet actually laughed to herself as she listened to their plans. They had no contingent in place to deal with Regina's magic. There was no magic in this realm (Regina was waiting to have Scarlet do magic training in her last realm before returning to Wonderland) so they weren't fully aware of how powerful it could be. Scarlet's guess was that they weren't even aware of it as being a weapon.

Scarlet didn't want to involve Regina if she didn't have to. She considered this to be a test of her intelligence. She hoped that if she could thwart this plan then it would be another step toward her being a good ruler. Also, she knew that even if she failed Regina would be able to handle them.

She continued to search the castle for anything that would help her stop this plot. She searched the library for any history on the Queen or her family that might help. Mostly she wanted to see if there was any history of magic in the family.

She found no mention of magic anywhere in the histories. Scarlet thought that was extremely suspicious. One thing she had learned from Regina was that every realm had some kind of magician in their histories. For a realm to have no history of magic was just not possible.

She continued searching the castle until she found a secret tunnel in the basement. It was a very small tunnel with just barely enough room for her to get through. Luckily it was a very short tunnel. At the end of it was a very old door that looked like it hadn't been opened in decades.

She managed to get it open but only by using magic. Inside she found hundreds of books. She scanned the first few briefly and found what she had been looking for; histories of magic within this realm. She read the oldest and the newest. The oldest told of the way magic was once a basic part of life in this realm. In the last book she read about the current Queen's magic.

She had been born with magic so strong that her first cry made all the flowers in the garden bloom and grow. The people of the realm rejoiced. Surely an infant's cry that could cause such growth meant she would be an impressive and wonderful Queen.

This book was a diary written by one of the advisors to the man who was the King when this

Queen was born. It ended with a not-so-pleasant entry. This Queen's youth had been all the realm hoped for and more. She protected them all and grew food with her magic so the realm would thrive.

Then when she was thirteen a stranger came to the realm. He wooed the young Queen. She fell madly in love with him. All the plans were in place for the wedding and the realm was joyous with their Queen's happiness. Then, the day before the wedding, the stranger vanished. The Queen was found sobbing and bleeding with her clothing torn. Nine months later she gave birth to her first son.

After his birth she erased the memory of magic, the stranger, and her youth from every mind in the realm. She gave them all new memories and new traditions to live by. Then she had all the books locked away. As a final measure she had the advisor who had written the journal locked in the room with the books to die.

Scarlet looked around the room but didn't see any bones. The advisor must have somehow escaped. Scarlet searched every nook and cranny until she found the escape route. She followed a very small tunnel hidden behind three removable wall stones. The tunnel took her out into the forest surrounding the palace. Not too far from where the tunnel let out she found a small cottage.

She sat and watched the cottage for a while. She could see movement inside. She used her magic to see how many people there were and found just one old man. So she went up to the door and knocked.

She was met by an old woman. She quirked her eyebrow at her. Her magic had clearly shown her an old man alone inside. She expected to be turned away but the woman stepped back and let her come inside. Once the door closed behind them she let the glamour fade so she was an old man.

He explained to Scarlet that he was the advisor who had been locked in that room. He had been the one to tell the Queen about that room when she wanted to hide the books. He had a feeling she would trap him there so he suggested a place he knew he could escape. He has been hiding in this cottage and watching the Queen ever since.

Scarlet spent hours there with the old advisor sharing secrets about the Queen. Between the two of them they came up with a plan to stop the Queen and her son. The Queen had another son, a boy of twelve, who would make a good ally. He loved his mother but was against her policies. He didn't want to take over other realms. He wanted to stay and make their realm a better place.

Scarlet sent word to Sharon and Anthony. They agreed to come help her. It would take them about a month to get there. In that time she would train the boy, Richard, on all the secrets of the realm. She

shared with him as many of the political lessons that
Anthony had shared with her as she could.

When Sharon and Anthony arrived, Scarlet
and Richard took them straight to the advisor's
cottage. They spent a few days there strategizing
before facing the Queen.

Facing the Queen was terrifying. She wielded
magic powerfully. She could grow flowers and plants
out of nothing. She could control them and make them
attack in any way she pleased. Unfortunately for the
Queen, Scarlet was from Wonderland. She had
spent her early years talking to plants and flowers.
With a whisper she could make them obey her.

The others weren't sure how to help. Anthony
had magic but he couldn't connect with these plants.
The advisor only knew how to glamour himself. He was
of no help.

While Scarlet and the Queen faced off,
Richard and Sharon worked their way toward the son

who was helping her. They were all hoping he was simply under a spell cast by the Queen and that once she was defeated he would be able to be reasoned with.

Scarlet managed to use the plants to wrap the Queen in a cocoon. The Queen's magic was too strong for Scarlet alone. She hadn't had enough training. The cocoon would hold her until Regina could get there to take care of her. She contacted Regina with her mirror and then sat to wait.

They tried to reason with the elder son while they waited but he fully believed in everything his mother had told him. Luckily they didn't have to wait long for Regina to arrive. She could travel just by stepping through mirrors.

Scarlet waited for her mother's wrath. She was certain she would be lectured about trying to handle this on her own. Regina sent the Queen and her son through the mirror to Wonderland. Going through the mirror stripped them of all magic. It took it from them and sent it out into the land and flowers.

Regina turned back to Scarlet and gave her an appraising look. Scarlet braced herself for yelling but instead Regina smiled. She congratulated her on her initiative. She also told her how smart she was to call for help when she realized she couldn't handle it on her own. She told her that was one of the marks of a great ruler.

She left Scarlet there to continue training Richard. Sharon and Anthony went back to their realms as well. This left Scarlet and the old advisor to teach Richard and his siblings.

She didn't stay long in this realm after that. She was just past sixteen when she left. The realm was in good hands and she still had so much more to learn.

Chapter Eleven

Regina had chosen the next realm carefully.
Scarlet was a woman now with a woman's body. They
didn't put much stock in monogamy in Wonderland. A
woman was free to have as many lovers as she wanted
and vice versa. This new realm had three sons and they
were all very handsome. Regina wanted Scarlet to
learn the art of seduction in this realm. Scarlet had
other ideas.

She knew she had plenty of time in her life to
learn about love. She simply wanted to learn and find
more allies. Unlike her mother she liked the idea of
monogamy. Finding one man to be her King and love
her for eternity. She wanted more than just a lover,
though. She wanted a partner.

The King and Queen of this land were very
vain people. They were both incredibly good looking
people. They put a lot of value on beauty. They took
to Scarlet immediately because she was incredibly

beautiful. She had incredible sea-green eyes and fire-red hair. Her body was perfectly proportioned. She was everything a man could want in a woman if they were going for looks alone.

The oldest and the youngest of the sons were vain like their parents. They placed a high value on looks as well. They didn't know much about their own kingdom. They hadn't bothered to learn. They believed the people would always love them for their looks.

The middle son, Dean, actually paid attention to what was going on in the kingdom. He took the time to get to know the people. He knew the policies of the government. He was doing what he could to keep the kingdom going before the rest of his family could destroy it.

Scarlet didn't trust him. His intentions seemed too good to be true. She couldn't bring herself to believe anyone could be that good hearted. So she watched him. She spied on him in secret as well as openly. She wanted him to know that she didn't trust him.

They circled around and around each other for a few months. In all of her spying she could find nothing that proved he was anything more than he appeared to be. He, on the other hand, had been spying on her as well and had learned nothing at all. He didn't know about her magic or her alliances. He didn't even know how intelligent she really was. He believed her to be another vapid, pretty face.

She was having a lot of fun toying with him. She knew he was spying and she played into that. It allowed her to get closer to him and learn his secrets. After those few months, though, she had to give in and admit that he really was as nice as he seemed. So she approached him to broker a truce.

She approached him in the library. He was reading a large volume on the politics of the next kingdom over. She asked him about it and he explained that his neighbor's crime rate was much lower than theirs. His parents didn't care much about what went on in the kingdom as long as everyone thought they were beautiful.

Dean wanted to try to incorporate some new policies into their own government. He just wasn't sure how to get his parents to do anything. This was where Scarlet found her opening. She began teaching him what she knew about indoctrinating politics. Together they came up with a plan that would allow him to actually rule the kingdom without his parents having to step aside. They just had to get them, and his older brother who was next in line, to go along with this.

There was a lot of arguing. His parents were confused by the entire idea and his brother was adamant that he would not be bossed around by his little brother. Once he started arguing, his parents put their foot down and insisted he give up on the idea.

In the end it was Scarlet who convinced them all. Although "convinced" was putting it nicely. She tried painting a pretty picture for them of how easy their lives would be. The brother still refused. Finally she put on a magic show for them.

She pretended to be extremely angry with their stupidity. She made her eyes flare red and her hair crackle with electricity. She let the crackle work its way down her arms and into her hands so that it looked like she was going to hurt them with it. She was breathing heavily and glaring at them. Then she took a deep breath and made herself look like she was visibly calming herself. She closed her hands around the sparks. She closed and opened her eyes very slowly so they were back to normal.

The King, Queen, and older brother were visibly scared. Dean just looked impressed. She was sure she had their attention now so she took another deep breath before continuing. She told them in no uncertain terms just what she thought of them. She threatened that if they continued to ruin their country with their shallowness then she would be forced to bring the weight of Wonderland down on them.

She pointed out to them that they had done nothing for their country in years. Really it was only the efforts of Dean that was keeping their kingdom going at all. They were so scared by her that they would probably have agreed to anything.

Scarlet stayed in this realm until she was eighteen. She worked closely with Dean to shape the realm into what she thought it should be. She stayed longer than she should to make sure the King and Queen weren't going to go back on their word. She also had the older brother sent to Wonderland.

In Wonderland Regina was using him as a toy. She was putting his good looks to use. She had him doing odd jobs throughout the realm for any woman who was willing to pay a large fee to have someone pretty do their work. Amazingly he loved the work. It kept him fit and active and he got to see a lot of interesting things around the realm.

All in all it seemed like the solution they had put into place was working wonderfully. It was time for Scarlet to move on.

Chapter Twelve

Scarlet spent the first week in the new realm reading through the diaries she had kept over the years. She was supposed to be learning different political policies and try to indoctrinate them into her own agenda in order to be a better queen. Instead it seemed like she hadn't learned anything since Anthony.

She had created allies and solved problems for others but she didn't see how that was going to help her in her own realm. Especially as she hadn't been able to solve a problem on her own since the first realm. And she had only been five then.

This new realm was supposed to be her final realm. In this realm she was to learn more about magic and how to control it. The royal family of this realm was not magical. They had a wizard on their council, though, who was said to be very powerful.

Regina had never actually met him. She had sent out inquiries to all the realms to ask who would be best to train her daughter and every response had come back with his name. She made all the arrangements with him via correspondence. Scarlet had also heard from each realm that he was the best and she was looking forward to her first lesson with him.

She was in the realm for three months before he scheduled her first lesson. He kept making excuses to push it back. Scarlet finally dropped a not-so-subtle hint that she would be writing to her mother soon. The next day he scheduled her first lesson.

They were only five minutes in when Scarlet realized he was a complete charlatan. She let the lesson continue through to the end without any indication she knew he was full of crap. She let him believe she fell for his act the way everyone else had.

When she left the lesson she went out into the woods with her little mirror. She contacted Regina. She expected her mother to say she would come deal with the man herself but she didn't. Instead she shocked Scarlet by telling her she already knew. She had been observing the man through the looking glass. She felt this would be a good lesson for Scarlet. She wanted her to handle it in whatever way she saw fit.

Regina told Scarlet that her first instinct to call for help was good but that she needed to take control now. Scarlet was flattered by her mother's confidence in her. She wanted to take some time with this, though, and figure out how to do it on her own.

She let the lessons continue so she could study the so-called wizard. She wanted to learn as much about him as she could in order to learn his weaknesses. She needed to find something she could exploit that would expose him to all the realms.

She used her mother's trick of observing him through the looking glass when after a couple of weeks of bogus lessons she hadn't learned anything. She was actually kind of surprised he hadn't thought to cover it when he was alone. Everyone knew about Regina and her looking glass. Apparently that connection had never occurred to him.

After a week of observing nothing interesting when he was alone she finally figured it out. She had noticed the chain he wore around his neck but never thought it could be anything unusual. Then one night a young girl from the village was brought to him so he could assess her powers. This was the custom for this realm and he had never been wrong.

There had been several young people in the realm who had been found to have strong magic. They were always sent to other realms to train as the wizard was too busy advising the King and Queen. Not everyone who came to be tested was found to be magical, though.

Scarlet watched as the young girl was brought in and left alone with him. He pulled the chain out from where it was tucked in his shirt and attached to it was a beautiful amulet. Scarlet gasped aloud when she saw it because she knew exactly what it was.

The amulet belonged in Wonderland. It was so old no one remembered its actual name. They simply called it the "lost treasure" now. Before Regina had come the amulet had been the source of magic in Wonderland. About twenty years before Regina's arrival it had been stolen. Without it Wonderland had started to die. Regina had saved them all.

Back then the amulet had a lot of power stored in it. Scarlet wasn't sure how he was getting the power out of the amulet though. However he was doing it, he couldn't be very good at it to be so inept. Unless he was faking that.

Scarlet watched as the charlatan held the amulet against the young girl's head. He said a couple of words and a rainbow of colors flared around the girl. Scarlet knew this was a way of reading someone's magic but he hadn't learned how to do that yet. Once he had read the rainbow he said a couple more words. Scarlet watched in horror as the rainbow left the girl and transferred into the amulet.

The girl collapsed to the floor. She was only unconscious for a few moments before regaining consciousness. The charlatan helped her to her feet and told her that the test for magic had found nothing magical about her. He sent her back out to her parents and sent them on their way.

Scarlet cancelled her lessons for the rest of the week. She claimed she wasn't feeling well. She didn't leave her room for the next three days. She needed some time to think about what to do. She ran a risk of him using the amulet on her if she confronted him head on. At the same time she worried that he had been using it on her little bits at a time.

The little girl didn't remember anything when she woke up. Who was to say he wasn't siphoning off her magic bits at a time during their lessons?

She was going to need to do more research on the amulet. She needed the history books from Wonderland.

Chapter Thirteen

The amulet was beautiful. It was shaped like a star. In the center was a large purple stone. The wizard who created it poured all of his magic into the stone. He named the amulet "Estrella". He then opened a portal to a land that did not yet exist.

His son discovered his body the next day. He also found his diary. In the diary he explained that he had been fighting with his magic all his life. It was too powerful for him and he was terrified of what was going to happen when he died. He was certain it would go out into the realm and hurt people if it wasn't contained. So he created the amulet and sent it to where it couldn't hurt anyone.

His son studied everything his father had left. He read about specific incidents that had happened because of his magic. His son agreed that it needed to be contained. He just wished his father could have done it without ending his own life.

He went through his diary extensively and found a way to reopen the portal to nowhere. He had to be sure the magic was actually contained. What he found instead was a new land. In the center of the land was a full grown and beautiful tree with the Estrella in the center of it.

The son was determined to cut the Estrella out of the tree and destroy it. He knew that any world created out of his father's magic like this had to be bad. He reached out and placed his hand on the Estrella in order to remove it but was flooded with visions. He saw the future of Wonderland and how it would all turn out. He couldn't destroy that kind of potential.

He stayed in Wonderland and began to write down all that he had seen. When he was hungry the strange creatures brought him food. When he was lonely the flowers sang to him and the trees spoke with him. His books ended with the arrival of Regina as the new ruler of Wonderland for that was as far as the Estrella had taken him. When he finished writing he gave the books to the trees then he laid down and died.

Through the magic of the Estrella the trees that read the books turned into people. Well, they became like people. They were what humans would call Elves. They lived peacefully in Wonderland until the magic of the Estrella was stolen. Then Wonderland became very ill. They were close to death when Regina arrived and saved them all.

Chapter Fourteen

Scarlet was actually scared about having to face the charlatan. She took some comfort in the fact that her mother believed she could handle this on her own. Still, she felt very vulnerable taking this on without any of her friends to help.

She had no idea how to even begin to face this problem. At first she thought that because she came from Wonderland that the Estrella wouldn't be able to take her magic. But then she ruled that out because her mom wasn't from Wonderland.

Then she thought that maybe it could only take weak magic. Not everyone who came to be tested was sent away as non-magical. The ones who were found to have magic and sent away to train were powerful enough that it would have been obvious to anyone. Her choices with this theory were that he either let them be because they were so powerful or because the amulet couldn't absorb that much power.

She didn't want to face him until she knew more. Unfortunately the diaries of the son had been lost long ago. All that was left was the basic story. She thought that maybe the charlatan had the original diaries; that he had taken them when he took the Estrella.

She knew they weren't in his office. He did all of his lessons in his office. She had been through every book he had and there weren't that many. If he had them they had to be somewhere else in the castle. It was time for her to start exploring.

It only took her two days to find them. Amazingly they were in the kitchen; disguised as cook books. She was able to sense the enchantment on the them and see them for what they were. She took them back up to her room and spent the entire night reading. And she found her answer.

When she was a young child in Wonderland she would wander in the woods. She knew the creatures would keep her safe because she was the Princess so she never worried about how far she went. On one of her explorations she found a magnificent tree.

This tree didn't talk like other Wonderland trees yet she could feel a consciousness coming from it. She felt an amazing sereneness coming from it. She climbed up into it and felt like she was being enveloped in a hug. As she sat there an Elf came out of the woods.

When the Estrella has been stolen the Elves turned themselves back into trees to survive. An Elf in Elf form was a very rare thing. Even as a child she knew that.

The Elf never said a word to her. Like the tree she could feel his consciousness and it felt calm and relaxing. He handed her a necklace. It was a small blue stone set in the middle of a silver flower. It was on a delicate silver chain. Once she had put it on he turned and vanished back into the woods. The magnificent tree she was sitting in seemed to let out a contented sigh.

She never took that necklace off. She had always felt like it was more than just jewelry though. Now she knew. When the Estrella had gone through the portal into nothingness a small part of the stone had fractured off. In the diaries it said that the small section would be found by the First Elf and crafted into a necklace; "the flower of Wonderland."

When the time was right the First Elf would present the necklace to the one who would bring the Estrella back to Wonderland. It had been written that this person would be the protector of Wonderland and would bring the original magic back.

Her mother had seen the necklace when she came back from the woods that day but never said a word about it. Now Scarlet knew where Regina's confidence in her had come from. She also now understood why she had really been sent out to learn politics from other realms. She was actually on a mission to find the Estrella.

Even now knowing she was meant to bring the Estrella home she was still trepidatious.

That night she was visited in her dreams by the First Elf. He explained to her about her heritage. He himself was her father and Regina's one true love. However, with the Estrella gone from Wonderland some of the trees believed he should have taken its place to save the magic. They knew Regina was coming but they were close to death and scared. They had started threatening him and he had gone into hiding.

He still kept himself hidden even after Regina's arrival because there were some who still wanted to use him. They felt that his magic combined with Regina's would create a new magic so powerful that it would make Wonderland the uncontested ruler of all the realms. In a way they had been right. But it hadn't been his and Regina's magic that had made something powerful. It had been their love. Because their love had created her.

Scarlet was special because her magic was a mixture of Estrella magic from the creation of Wonderland and Regina magic which was the only one that could save a dying Wonderland. The Estrella couldn't hurt her because she was part of it. There was nothing the charlatan could do to hurt her.

The First Elf told her he had been watching her all her life. He was very impressed with the way she was able to read people and make friends. He told her that once she returned to Wonderland he believed she would build a brighter future than he ever imagined. She would be able to unite the realms without dominating them. He told her to believe in her compassionate heart.

When she woke, the stone in her necklace was glowing. She knew exactly what she needed to do. She went directly to the charlatan's chamber. He was in the middle of "testing" a young boy who had been brought to him. She walked right up to him and tore the chain right off his neck. Without the amulet the charlatan turned back into a Wonderland flower.

Scarlet did a quick bit of magic so that the flower was in a pot and wouldn't die. She carried the flower down to the King and Queen and explained the situation to them. They gave her permission to take the flower back to Wonderland to be dealt with. Scarlet was happy to finally be going home.

Chapter Fifteen

The flower had been given the Estrella by an Elf who had pried it from the tree. The Elf had lost her love and wanted Wonderland to die with him. So she gave the Estrella to her favorite flower. The Estrella had turned the flower into a man. The Elf opened a portal and sent the flower and Estrella out of Wonderland.

The Elf had been furious when Regina arrived and saved Wonderland. Regina was so beloved that the Elf knew she'd never get close enough to hurt her. So she turned herself back into a tree and let her grief take her.

Now with the Estrella back she left her tree state to try to confront Regina. She stormed into the castle intent on hurting Regina and thereby hurt Wonderland. Instead of Regina she came face to face with Scarlet.

Scarlet had put the amulet around her own neck before stepping through the portal back to Wonderland so that she could carry the flowerpot with her hands. Somewhere in the portal the Estrella and her flower necklace had fused. It had created a whole new amulet. Scarlet still wore it around her neck.

When the Elf saw the new amulet she stepped back in shock. Tears dripped down her face as she asked Scarlet about it. She then shocked Scarlet by telling her that her love's last words to her had been to look for the Scarlet Rose. The amulet around Scarlet's neck was shaped like an exquisite rose bloom.

The Elf, Isabella, fell to the ground crying. When she was finally able to control herself to speak she told Scarlet of the last words of her love. He was dying from having eaten a poisonous plant. He had puller her near to him and told her that she would find love again when the Scarlet Rose bloomed in

Wonderland. She had thought his words to be from some kind of hallucination caused by the plant. Now, seeing Scarlet standing before her, she had hope.

Scarlet was completely taken by the Elf's beauty; made all the more alluring by the happiness now lighting up her face. Without any other thought than of Isabella's beauty, she pulled her into her arms and kissed her passionately. When her brain caught up with her actions she pulled back with an apology on her lips. One look at Isabella's face and the words die in her throat. She had never seen such pure joy before.

They heard an embarrassed sounding cough behind them and turned to see they were being watched by Regina and the First Elf. Isabella immediately dropped into a bow. Scarlet wasn't sure what to do. She knew Elves care nothing for gender rules; especially the Elves of Wonderland as they had never been part of a society that had any rules. She was worried about what Regina's reaction would be. After all, she was the future ruler of Wonderland.

Scarlet held her breath as she waited for Regina's ire. Instead, Regina smiled and asked if Scarlet's guest would join them for dinner.

Wonderland was thriving again now that the Estrella was returned. Regina's magic had kept Wonderland alive but there had been no new growth. Now that the Estrella was back the land was thriving.

Regina agreed that there was no hurry for Scarlet to take over ruling Wonderland. The First Elf assured them both that she didn't have to keep the Estrella in Wonderland for the magic to thrive. She could leave the realm still wearing it and the magic would still grow.

So Scarlet decided to travel to other realms. She still felt that there was a lot to learn before she was ready to take over. She and Isabella left Wonderland together to study. They were in the realm where Alex had met Beth, studying in the University, when Alex first laid eyes on Scarlet.

Chapter Sixteen

Alex came back to the University every so often to try to re-create the magic they had. He had enrolled in the University to study literature this time. He went into the library to get a book for one of his courses when he saw Scarlet sitting at one of the tables. She had books all around her and was writing maniacally into a notebook.

He completely lost himself for a moment as he stared at her. He almost went against every technique he had ever used and walked over and started a conversation with her. He was actually halfway across the room before he came to his senses. He walked past her and went to a table on the other side of the room where he could watch her without being obvious.

She worked very intently. He was very impressed by the look of determination on her face as she flipped through books and wrote out notes. He wanted to learn everything there was to know about her. So he left the library and went back to his dorm so he could watch her through the looking glass. This was where he found his first obstacle. He couldn't see her in the looking glass.

He had never not been able to see whoever he wanted. Spying through the looking glass had been the way he had won every woman he had ever married. Without that edge he wasn't sure what to do next.

He knew he should walk away right then and there. Someone who couldn't be seen through the looking glass had to be a very powerful enchantress. He couldn't help it though. He saw her face every time he closed his eyes. He just had to get to know this woman. So he started following her.

He was very careful not to be obvious. He didn't want to scare her and he certainly didn't want to invoke her wrath. If she was as powerful as he was assuming she was then she could probably end his life with a word. Obviously he didn't want to take that chance.

She rarely left campus. When she did she was always accompanied by another woman. Something about the other woman seemed familiar to him but he was so concentrated on Scarlet he didn't give it much thought. The first time he heard Scarlet's name he thought it was the most wonderful thing he had ever heard. Her hair was the most amazing shade of red that no other name could possibly have suited her.

After a couple of weeks of following her around and trying to learn as much as he could about her, he reached the point where he felt he couldn't wait any longer. He just had to talk to her. So he approached her in the library and tried to strike up a conversation. She turned him away quickly but was very polite about it. He decided to take that as a good sign.

A few days later he ran into her in a local coffee shop. She was with the girl that he had often seen her with on campus. He decided to try talking with her again. He went over to where the two girls were sitting and pulled up a chair to join them. He tried to start a conversation that included both of them but they were almost frosty in trying to get him to leave.

He took the rejection well and left their table. He sat himself across the room from them and with this back to them so they wouldn't think he was a stalker. Luckily for him a friend from one of his classes joined him right after he sat down so he wouldn't be tempted to keep turning around to look. He felt a draw to Scarlet that he had never felt for any woman before.

He continued to watch her for the next few days. He was looking for another opening to talk to her. It almost seemed like she was avoiding him. Every time he spotted her she would turn and go the other way.

It was a month before he finally got her alone to talk. They were actually having a very nice conversation. He learned that she was studying political sciences. She was hoping to someday make a change in the government of her country.

Up close she was even more beautiful than he could have imagined. When they parted at the end of the conversation his heart was full. He had fallen deeply in love with her. He decided to bring her chocolates the next day. He didn't want to portal back to Wonderland, though, so he got them in town. He was sure he had his heart in his eyes when he gave them to her.

She was really nice about her refusal to accept them. She insisted that she didn't like chocolate. They had another pleasant conversation and he walked away even more in love. Somehow he was going to have to win her heart.

He spent the rest of the semester trying to win her affections. He knew that she was starting to regard him as a friend but he wanted more. He had been as charming as he could possibly be but she just wasn't falling. He didn't understand it until one day he came across her in the back of the library. She was with the girl that she spent so much time with. They were back there kissing where no one else could see them.

He knew if he was going to have a chance with her he was going to have to get her away from that girl. He thought that maybe if he took her away to Wonderland that she could fall for him. So, he started working on his plans to get her alone and portal her to Wonderland.

Once there he would have her all to himself in the manor. He knew there was no way she could not fall for him. He'd had so many wives before and he'd won every one of them. Plus he had the nectar that would make her compliant.

He told her he had found a new species of flower in the woods behind the campus. He asked her if she would come with him to look at it. He told her he was hoping to be named a discoverer in a scientific journal. He got her a little ways into the woods and then he opened a portal. He grabbed ahold of her and pulled her through it into the gardens of his manor home.

He expected her to look around in awe and start talking to the flowers like every other woman had. Instead she screamed. She turned on him and started striking every part of him she could reach. He finally had to blow sleeping powder in her face that he had gotten from a distant land. She fell into an instant sleep. He carried her inside and laid her down on his bed. He had to take a little time to think about what to do now.

Chapter Seventeen

Isabella was frantic. She knew Scarlet was going for a walk with Alex to look at some kind of new flower. But that was hours ago. She couldn't see any sign of either of them anywhere.

Isabella had never liked Alex. She could tell that he had a thing for Scarlet but Scarlet couldn't see that. She thought he was just being friendly because like them he was from "another country". Scarlet had taken pity on him and had been friendly. Now they were both gone and Isabella was certain he had something to do with it.

So, she was shocked when she saw him in the library the next day. When she confronted him, he insisted that Scarlet had never shown up for their walk. He said he had seen her on campus talking agitatedly with some guy he had never seen before. They seemed to be having a heated discussion so he walked away.

Isabella didn't believe him but since she couldn't prove anything she walked away. Back in their dorm room she pulled out the looking glass and started calling all of Scarlet's friends. When all of them told her they hadn't seen or heard from her she went back to Wonderland to see Regina.

She was terrified that Regina was going to blame her for her daughter's disappearance. She was trembling from head to toe as she stood before her. Once again the Queen's reaction shocked her. Instead of yelling or blaming Isabella she tried to comfort her. She insisted that it wasn't her fault and that if someone had been that intent on taking her, they would have found a way no matter what. She also told Isabella that she was lucky that whoever did this, did it without hurting her.

Isabella was grateful for the way Regina was treating her. It made her feel like family. Regina included her in everything she did as she began investigating Scarlet's disappearance.

They sat together and went over every detail of the life they had been leading on campus. Isabella gave full descriptions of everyone they interacted with regularly. Isabella noticed that Regina seemed to be particularly interested in Alex. She asked a lot of questions about him and was especially interested in the details he gave about what he saw before the missed walk.

Regina asked Isabella if she would take her to see Alex. She told Isabella she had a suspicion about Alex's identity and she wanted to prove she was right. So they went through a portal together back to the campus. Isabella took Regina to every place on campus she knew Alex would go.

When they didn't find him anywhere, Regina asked Isabella if she would mind accompanying her on a hunch. They portalled back to Wonderland and

Regina led Isabella to Alex's manor. Isabella gave
Regina a quizzical look and asked why they were at
the Hatter's manor. Regina explained that Isabella's
description of Alex matched the Hatter.

Isabella had never actually met the Hatter.
She had heard stories of him and his penchant for
repeatedly getting married. Everyone knew about
that. But he had never stolen a wife before.

Alex opened the door to his manor house with
a look of surprise at seeing Regina there. His
surprised look became almost comical when Isabella
stepped out from behind Regina. He almost looked
like he was going to faint when he heard Scarlet is
Regina's daughter.

He stepped aside and let them in to look
around. He went out and took a seat in the garden
while they searched his house for signs of Scarlet.
When they didn't find anything he asked them if there
was anything he could do to help them find her.

When they left the manor, Isabella looked back to see Alex watching them. She couldn't understand why but she had the weirdest feeling that Scarlet was there somewhere. She needed to find some way to get back in there when he wasn't expecting it.

Chapter Eighteen

Alex watched them walk away and then closed the door. How could he have possibly missed the fact that Scarlet was Regina's daughter? Or even that Regina had a daughter? And Isabella. Seen here in Wonderland it was obvious that she was an Elf. How could he have missed that?

It was too late now to change anything. He had Scarlet hidden in a room in the back of the manor that was only accessible to him. Her being Regina's daughter explained why his nectar wasn't working on her. He was having to give her small doses of the sleeping powder; not enough to knock her out but just enough to keep her from escaping.

After the Queen and the Elf had left he sat down to try to think of what to do next. He knew that logically he should let her go and beg her not to tell her mother it was him who took her. But he was too far gone in love with her to think logically. He needed to find some way to make her love him back.

Her being a child of Wonderland complicated things drastically. He had no real magic of his own and her being Regina's child meant she had to have some kind of magic. He just had no idea how strong her magic was and couldn't take any chances lessening the drugs so he could find out.

He let himself into the room where he was keeping her. He sat in the chair facing the bed where she was laying. She looked over at him with loathing in her eyes. He studied her features to see if he could see any signs of Regina there. As he looked he noted similarities in the shape of her eyes and mouth. He also noticed that her ears had a very slight point to the tops suggesting that her father was an Elf.

He knew that Regina had had several lovers over the years but none of them had been an Elf. On top of that, how could she have gone through an entire pregnancy and raised a child to this age without him ever having known about it?

He left the manor then and started working his way through Wonderland. He asked everyone he knew about Scarlet. Many were clueless, like him, about her existence. He finally tracked down someone who worked in the castle when Scarlet was a child.

He learned of her childhood spent in other realms. He learned that she had made allies and friends everywhere she went. He learned that she had some magic but that she wasn't as strong as Regina. The only thing he learned about her that worried him was the identity of her father.

He'd had a run-in with the First Elf once. He had been out in the woods looking for plants to use in his nectars. The First Elf had come across him as he was digging up an unusual looking flower. He wanted to take it back to his manor to study it as he had never seen anything like it before. The First Elf had been livid. He threw him across the clearing using magic.

Alex had never gone back to that part of the woods again. He knew that Elves were powerful because their magic came from Wonderland itself. But he had never encountered magic as strong as what the First Elf possessed.

He went to Regina's castle to offer his help with the search. He wanted to stay as close to the investigation as possible. He hoped this way he could stay one step ahead of them. This way if he knew they were getting close he could move her. He thought that maybe he should take her to the palace of the wives. For now, though, she was fine where she was. Regina had already searched his manor.

He went back to the manor that evening and prepared a nice meal for Scarlet. He brought it to her and sat to talk to her while she ate. He told her how much he had fallen for her. He apologized to her for having taken her this way. He explained that he knew if he could just get her alone for a while then she could fall for him too.

She glared at him but never said a word. She hadn't spoken to him once since he had brought her here. He found it a bit frustrating but was willing to be as patient as he had to in order to win her heart.

He watched her as she ate. She kept furtively looking at the door. He knew that she was thinking if she could just get out the door she would be free. He was glad that the door was enchanted to only open to his touch. He had paid a lot of money to a traveling magician for that enchantment. He knew it worked because Regina hadn't found the room on her search.

Alex wanted to find a way to connect with Scarlet that would make her see him as something other than a captor. He brought her books and trinkets. He brought her candy and flowers. He did everything he could to make the room feel like a home to her. Nothing he did seemed to make her any happier.

He had her in the room for a month before she spoke to him. He was pretty sure it was just because the solitude was getting to her. He would take it, though. Getting her to talk to him was the only way he was going to win her heart.

She asked him if he was going to keep her locked away like this for the rest of her life or if she could at least have a Wonderland flower to keep her company. He agreed to bring her one and then promised that once it was safe he would take her to the Palace of the Wives. Her eyes widened when she heard that and he realized that she hadn't figured out before that he was the Hatter.

He didn't know if it was pure curiosity then or just an attempt to trick him into telling her something about himself that she could use against him, but she started asking him questions about himself. She told him that her mom had warned her about the Hatter when she was young. She told him her mom had said that he was never really serious about his relationships and would never truly fall in love.

As she said that he saw the despair fill her eyes as her mother's remembered words took all of her hope. He tried to reassure her that this time was different. This time he was truly in love and he would never leave her. She insisted then that she was tired and turned her back on him to go to sleep.

Chapter Nineteen

When Scarlet woke the next day it was to Alex bringing her a Wonderland flower in a pot. It was a beautiful rose that was the same shade as her hair. She smiled at the flower.

She thought to herself that Alex should have known she was from Wonderland just by the color of her hair. It was a red that only showed up in Wonderland. It was proof that she was a true child of the place.

As soon as he left her alone with the flower she began to whisper to it. She told it a story about her childhood that the flowers would remember so she could prove who she was. The flower told her that wasn't necessary. She still wore the Scarlet Rose amulet. The flower couldn't do anything while in the room but promised that as soon as she was out she would spread the word. She would help get Scarlet back to where she belonged.

The rose was with her for a couple of weeks before Alex swapped it out for a Tiger Lily. Scarlet had a lot of hope that it wouldn't be long before she was rescued. Two weeks went by and the Tiger Lily was replaced with a Hyacinth. Two more weeks and the Hyacinth was replaced with a Tulip. Scarlet began to lose hope of ever leaving this room.

Then one day out of the blue Alex led her out of the room. He took her out to his carriage and they headed away from the manor. He took her all the way to the other side of Wonderland. She saw the Palace loom up in front of her and realized he was taking her to the Palace of the Wives.

She felt a glimmer of hope that quickly turned to frustration. It became obvious after only a couple of days that the wives were completely loyal to Alex. There was no way they were going to help her escape. They wouldn't even let her talk to the flowers alone. She began to suspect that the ones that had kept her company had been done away with once they'd left her room.

After a week she became so despondent that she stopped leaving her room. It was so frustrating to be so close to home and not be able to get there. Somehow Alex was keeping her magic suppressed so she couldn't save herself. She cried herself to sleep each night thinking she would be stuck in this predicament forever.

She has been shut away in her self-imposed isolation for about a week when through the window she could hear the flowers start to sing. It was a slow and sweet song about the Estrella. As the music from the garden began to fade she felt like she could still hear it. She realized that the flowers outside the garden had started singing as well. They were carrying the tune across Wonderland.

She smiled to herself as she realized she hadn't been abandoned at all. The flowers had simply needed time to think of a way to get the message out without the wives realizing what was happening. She had figured out early on that Alex didn't know about the Estrella or what it truly was. Otherwise he would have taken the Scarlet Rose from her.

She could hear the music growing fainter as it made its way across Wonderland. She knew the First Elf would understand what it meant but she had no idea how it would lead him back to her. Her brain was too foggy to comprehend that the flowers would be able to lead them to her.

She laid down and fell asleep while the melody of the song played in her head.

Chapter Twenty

The First Elf was the first to notice the music as it approached them. It moved through the flowers as if through a wave. They all came together to listen to the song as it came near.

Regina had been amassing an army. She was sure that Scarlet was somewhere in Wonderland and even more sure that Hatter had something to do with her disappearance. She had searched his manor house and the Palace of the Wives and hadn't found her or any sign of her in any place. Of course, he could have been ferrying her between the two before Regina's search.

Regina had pulled together every ally that Scarlet had made. She had also brought the Elves out of hiding. Every creature who could help in any way had also come to the castle to prepare for the rescue. The castle had been a very busy and noisy place.

Now as the music grew closer everything stopped. Every creature, Elf, and ally turned their focus on the music. The First Elf smiled a huge grin when he was finally able to make out the words of the song.

The Estrella grows weak

Though her power is strong

Surrounded by enemies

Although not for long

Her lover will come

To take her away

The Estrella will free those

Held in nectar's sway

The Estrella will blossom

To a beautiful Rose

She'll make Wonderland whole again

And defeat nectar's throes

The Estrella she waits

For her lover to come

And once reunited

The battle's begun

The First Elf turned to Regina. She looked a little confused. He realized she didn't know about the nectar the Hatter gave his wives to make them complacent. Regina's look of confusion turned to a look of horror as she realized what this meant for Scarlet. The First Elf calmed her by explaining a nectar created using items found in Wonderland, as this was, would not work on a child of Wonderland.

Regina turned to the crowd who was amassed at the castle. This was no group of warriors but every bit would help. They had no idea what they would be facing. But at least now they knew where they were going.

The Palace of the Wives.

It took them some time to get coordinated. They had everything all set for a battle. They just really hoped it wouldn't come to that.

They made it into the garden at the Palace before they saw any signs of life. Once inside all of the wives came out and blocked every entrance to the actual Palace. When Regina demanded they take her to her daughter they looked scared but determined to keep her out.

When Isabella stepped forward to try to reason with them, they took this as a sign to attack. Then all hell broke loose.

The battle had been going strong for about ten minutes before the Hatter joined in. He had a sword that was enchanted to deflect magic. He was doing a pretty good job of throwing everything back at Regina and her followers.

Regina had just thrown a ball of energy at the Hatter when one of the wives jumped in front of him to protect him. When the energy hit her she dropped like a stone. Alex dropped his sword and fell to his knees beside her. He pulled her into his arms and cradled her head into his lap. He looked around and saw several of his wives laying sprawled on the ground.

He looked up into Regina's eyes. Without a word she understood that he was giving up. He turned his attention to Isabella and told her where to find Scarlet. Regina let out a sigh of relief. Finally it was over and she was going to get her daughter back.

Chapter Twenty One

When Isabella entered the room she was cautious. She wasn't sure what she was going to find. She had been with Alex for quite a while and it was possible he had found a way to brainwash her. So she very slowly walked to where Scarlet was staring out the window and whispered her name to her.

When she turned, Isabella could see the surprise on Scarlet's face. Scarlet very tentatively reached out a hand to touch Isabella. Then she threw herself into Isabella's arms and sobbed into her chest. Isabella held her and stroked her hair while whispering words of comfort to her.

When they walked out of the Palace together everyone cheered. Well, everyone except the wives. They looked angry. Some looked downright murderous. Regina had Hatter's hands bound with lengths of tough vines. He looked downtrodden and defeated. When his eyes met Scarlet's they filled with tears. His love for her was obvious.

The First Elf was going to stay behind to try to sort things out with the wives and figure out what should be done with them.

Regina kept the Hatter bound when she seated him in the carriage. She was going to lock him in the dungeons back in her castle until she and Scarlet could decide what to do with him. Just as Isabella had been worried, Regina was worried that Scarlet would want to be lenient due to feelings she may have developed for her captor. If it were strictly up to her she would have him beheaded. She wanted to let Scarlet be part of the decision, though, as a way to help her start to heal.

When they got back to the castle, Regina personally took the Hatter down to the dungeons. She knew that as the Queen she should interview him to find out why he had done it. She should listen to his justifications and try to take his state of mind into account before sentencing. She knew this was the rational thing to do but she was just too angry to even look at him.

She locked him in a cell and used unbreakable vines, a magic she had perfected over the years specifically for use in place of the locks in the cells in the dungeons, to secure the door. She left four guards, two facing the cell and two on either side of the door with their backs to the wall, and went in search of Scarlet.

She found her sitting in the kitchen with Isabella. She was picking distractedly at a cookie. They were sitting in silence. Regina thought this was odd until Isabella exhaled a relieved sigh and explained that Scarlet was waiting for her before talking because she only wanted to tell the story once.

Scarlet took a deep breath and explained it all from the trip into the woods to see the non-existent new flowers to the moment Isabella entered her room at the Palace. Isabella let out an angry hiss when she heard the part about the secret room at the manor. They had been so close to her but had no idea she was there.

Regina realized as she listened that Scarlet blamed herself for two reasons. The first was that she felt she should have realized from the first meeting that Alex was from Wonderland. Regina was able to calm that thought by explaining the Hatter's history to her. After all, he wasn't actually from Wonderland.

Scarlet's second reason for blaming herself was that she felt she should have been able to escape using magic. She was a child of Wonderland and had the amulet that had been the beginning of it all. Surely this should have made her strong enough to escape using magic; especially being that they were in Wonderland. She knew she was being drugged somehow but she still felt she should have been able to overcome that with her magic.

Regina reminded her that she wasn't very strong with her magic yet. Yes, she was very powerful but magic was like a muscle; it had to be worked and strengthened. If she had tried to use it without knowing what she was doing and while in her drugged state she could have ended up hurting herself.

Scarlet listened to this defense but still looked as if she didn't fully believe it. Regina promised her that whether she decided to stay in Wonderland or go back to the University, they would start working on training her in magic. She brightened with that statement and Regina realized it wasn't just the promise of magic training that made her smile; it was also the realization that she was still going to be allowed the freedom to make her own choices.

Scarlet had been sitting there waiting for Regina to tell her that she had to stay in Wonderland.

She had worried that her dreams of learning the best ways to rule would be dashed by the kidnapping. She had feared that her mother would have decided she was in too much danger on her own. Regina assured her that it was just an odd string of events that had led to her and the Hatter being in the same place at the same time.

But now they had bigger concerns to worry about. Regina wanted Scarlet to take a few days to recoup and then together they would have to decide what to do about the Hatter.

Chapter Twenty Two

A week went by before Regina would even talk to Scarlet about the Hatter. She wanted to make sure that Scarlet gave the entire matter careful consideration before delivering a sentence.

When they first sat down to discuss it, Regina began with a reminder of the wives. This had been the one thing to keep Regina from immediately calling for his execution. She knew that if something were to happen to him the wives would be left on their own. And without the nectar that he gave them they would surely wake to the reality of what he had done to them. Regina worried that this sudden plunge back into reality would cause them to start a war.

There had never been a war in Wonderland. In fact, the closest thing to a war to ever happen there had been when Isabella had come to the castle. Even that had worked itself out without progressing to a battle. Even the "battle" at the Palace of the Wives had ended so quickly it could only really be called a skirmish.

They spent days deliberating. There had been no word from the First Elf and that was starting to make them uneasy. They had sent messengers but they had never returned. The First Elf had the looking glass blocked so they couldn't get through to him that way either. They finally decided they were going to have to move forward without him.

They had decided to exile him from Wonderland. Scarlet, Regina, and Isabella worked together to create a spell. They then whispered the spell to a leaf taken from the Magic Tree of Wonderland. This leaf would then be placed upon the Hatter's chest; over his heart. It would imprint itself into his skin like a tattoo. The magic would penetrate his heart. This spell would make it so that once he left Wonderland he would never be able to return.

Scarlet had put together a trunk for him with things he would need once he was out of Wonderland. She had filled it with clothing, money, and paperwork he would need to start a new life. Regina and Isabella thought she was mad to do this but once she explained herself they found that her reasoning was sound.

Even though he had kidnapped her, he had been kind to her. He had made sure she was fed and warm. He brought her gifts and flowers for companionship. He had talked with her and tried to make her love him. But never once had he forced himself on her. He hadn't touched her or kissed her. He had been a gentleman and for that she was grateful.

She also hoped that by showing this kindness that he wouldn't be broken. She feared that exiling him would turn him against women and make him a monster. She had hope that given even the smallest second chance he would redeem himself. But she did agree that he couldn't be allowed to stay in Wonderland.

Regina brought him up from the dungeon so he could face Scarlet as she passed sentence on him. Regina felt that being the one to exile him would help Scarlet be able to put it all behind her.

Alex never took his eyes off her as she spoke. Regina could see that his obsession hadn't lessened at all. He looked disappointed at being exiled but she could see that he had hope when he saw the generosity she was showing with the trunk. There was no way he could come back but Regina feared he had hope Scarlet's kindness meant she would join him.

They had him strapped to a table and were ready to perform the spell when the doors opened and the First Elf came in. He was followed by an Elf that Regina thought looked familiar even though she was sure that she had never seen her before. They both demanded that they stop before the spell was enacted.

The mystery Elf went over to Alex and helped him sit up. He was staring at her with shock and wonder on his face. The First Elf pulled the others away to explain the situation. The mystery Elf was Alice.

Chapter Twenty Three

There never had been a real Alice. At least not a human one. This Elf, whose name really was Alice, had seen the Hatter from afar and thought he was the most handsome creature she had ever seen. She came forward as the young human who had "wandered" into Wonderland. She did everything she could to make him fall for her.

What was more, there had never been other wives. Once he had picked his woman to woo, Alice would go in and trade places with the girl. She was especially adept at glamour spells and could make herself look like anyone. She would pay off the woman to disappear until Alex was ready to go back to Wonderland.

Whenever Alex came to the Palace of the Wives, Alice would use sprites to make it look like there were multiple women there. Scarlet was the first time he had brought another person to Wonderland.

Alice hadn't tried to step in as he made his attempts to court her. She had seen Scarlet turn him down plenty of times. She had also seen Scarlet and Isabella together. She had never dreamed that Alex would kidnap her. He had never been forcible with a woman before. If they weren't willing he would move on.

Alice had come to the castle now to plead with Regina to let Alex stay in Wonderland. Alice couldn't live for long outside of Wonderland and she didn't want to be without him.

They listened to her story and her impassioned plea for him. Scarlet felt bad for her but still felt it was necessary for him to leave Wonderland. She would not feel safe with him still there. On top of that, what kind of ruler would she be if someone could kidnap her and not be punished?

Amazingly, Alice agreed. She asked Scarlet that the punishment be altered a little. Her request was that they alter the spell. He would still be in exile but his exile would be the confines of the Palace of the Wives. If he tried to leave the grounds he would become deathly ill. If he was off the grounds for more than five minutes he would die.

Scarlet pulled Regina and Isabella aside to discuss this request. Scarlet was moved by Alice's devotion. She had gone through so much for so long just to keep the love of her life. Scarlet felt that her request was reasonable. Plus it would allow them to keep an eye on him. Regina and Isabella agreed with that logic. However, they let the First Elf be the one to alter the spell.

The four of them circled around the Hatter. The First Elf placed the leaf over his heart. The four of them together said the words of the spell. Then Regina opened a portal and allowed Alice to take the Hatter back to the Palace.

Chapter Twenty Four

Once the portal closed and Alice was alone with Alex, she turned on him. It was obvious that she was angry and he was terrified of her. He had been with this woman for years under the guise of many personalities.

The fact that she had loved him enough to go through all of that should have given him some comfort. But he was afraid that him having put them in danger by kidnapping Scarlet may have ruined that love. He wanted to plead with her to forgive him and mostly not to hurt him.

Instead of yelling at him, though, she started in on a tirade about Scarlet. She fumed over Scarlet's refusal of him. She seemed to take it personally that Scarlet had chosen Isabella over Alex. How dare she thin k he wasn't good enough for her? She sounded like a lunatic as she raved. When she finally turned her attention to him she only had one question. What were they going to do to overthrow Regina and her precious little princess?

Alex let Alice rant for a while before reminding her he was stuck at the Palace for the rest of his life. She just waved him off and continued ranting. Alex sat himself down and let her rant until she wore herself out. He convinced her to go to bed and that they could talk about it with fresh minds. Really, he was just hoping that a good night's sleep would make her see reason.

He slept late the next morning. When he got up he found her sitting in the garden. She seemed calm. He couldn't see any sign of the lunatic ranting of the night before. He asked her if she would like to spend the day going through the Palace with him and deciding what kind of changes to make now that it was just the two of them. She smiled a little and told him they needed to spend the day strategizing.

He gave her a quizzical look. That's when she dropped the bombshell on him. While the Queen and her precious daughter had been consulting on her proposal, she had done a little sleight of hand and switched the leaves. She had swapped it out for a regular leaf that she had glamoured to look the one they had taken from the Magic Tree. The one they had used had absolutely no magical properties and was therefore useless.

He stared at her in shock. He was free to leave? He wouldn't be stuck spending the rest of his life here at the Palace? He sat down with her and eagerly began the discussion on how to overthrow them and take their places as the new Rulers of Wonderland. After all, Alice had more of a claim than Regina did. Alice had been brought to life with the magic that first started Wonderland. She was more fit to rule it.

Between the two of them they came up with a plan to take control of Wonderland. The hardest part, they thought, would be finding allies. Most of Wonderland was loyal to Regina and her daughter. Alice was sure she could count on the sprites and there were some creatures she thought might join them. Other than that, they were on their own.

They were going to sneak into Regina's castle in the night while everyone was sleeping. They were going to use some of Alex's sleeping powder on Regina, Scarlet, and Isabella so they wouldn't wake up. Once they were certain that they were deeply asleep, they would open a portal to nowhere and then push them through it. They would never be able to return.

They waited until it was late enough at night that even the flowers were asleep. Then they crept through the land to Regina's castle. They crept inside without seeing anything. It was very dark inside. They made it to the main hall before everything lit up like it was the middle of the day.

They turned in a circle in the center of the room to see that they were surrounded. Alex didn't have any magic but he did have his sword. Alice had magic and she refused to go down without a fight. They had no hope of winning but they started fighting anyway.

Isabella went for Alice first. They were locked in an intense magical battle that drew all other eyes to them. Somehow Alice managed to open the portal to nowhere and she was intent on trying to push Isabella through it. As they struggled the First Elf made his way quietly over to Alex. He put his hand on his chest and whispered a word of magic.

Alex collapsed to the ground dead. Alice turned just in time to see it happen and let out an agonized scream. With her distracted, Isabella was able to grab her and push her through the portal. She didn't go without a fight, though. She clung to Isabella and dragged her through the portal with her. Before anyone could react, the portal closed.

Part

Two

It all started with Alice. And for Scarlet it all ended with Alice too. When she dragged Isabella through the portal, she took Scarlet's heart with her. Now she was left trying to fix the mess Alice had made.

Chapter Twenty Five

It had been twenty years since that night. Scarlet had devoted herself to the study of politics across every realm. She had blended together several different political styles so that she could attack any problem from several different angles. She was proud of how smoothly things were going in Wonderland.

She kept herself so busy there was no time to be lonely. She turned the Palace of the Wives into a school. There they taught children and adults, sprites and fairies, and anyone who wanted to learn. They brought in exchange students from other realms. Scarlet and Regina both taught classes on politics.

Scarlet held weekly forums at the castle that allowed every inhabitant of Wonderland to have an audience with her. She let them air their grievances and listened to their ideas on how to make Wonderland better.

Every year she threw a huge party at the castle to celebrate Wonderland. Everyone in the realm was invited to attend. It was always the event of the year and always followed by a couple of weeks of incredible peace.

Not that Wonderland had any issues with that. Scarlet was so proactive as a ruler that everyone knew if they had issues they could go to her and she would help.

Regina worried about Scarlet. She never succumbed to depression. Regina feared the only reason for that, though, was that she kept herself so busy. She just wished she would open her heart and allow herself to love again.

There had been many hopefuls over the years but Scarlet never let any of them get close. She had grown very adept at turning them away but still keeping them as friends. It seemed like she had allies in every realm. Regina was proud of the way she managed the realm though.

It seemed like the realm was in a peaceful lull. They had all fallen into a routine and were all content. Until the stranger showed up.

Chapter Twenty Six

On first look he wasn't much to look at. His hair was a dull brown. His eyes were green but an olive drab kind of green. There was nothing remarkable about his face. He had an average build. He wasn't at all imposing or impressive in any way.

He came as an exchange student to the school. He was quiet in classes and kept to himself outside of them. He probably could have gone through his entire time at the school without being noticed if it weren't for the written work he turned in.

Regina brought his writing to Scarlet's attention. Regina had assigned her students to write a paper in which they created their own government. His paper had been creative but practical. He seemed to follow a lot of the policies that Scarlet herself believed. Scarlet was so impressed by the paper that she invited him to come to the castle for a private meeting with her.

Even his name was unassuming; John. It made Scarlet think of how unidentifiable people were called John Doe.

They had a pleasant meeting. They spoke of the politics of the different realms. They gave each other hypothetical situations to see how the other would work through them. The meeting went for much longer than either of them had planned. They probably would have continued talking long into the night if they didn't both have to get over to the school for other obligations. Scarlet invited him to return anytime he had time in his schedule.

For the first time in twenty years Scarlet felt hope. Here was a man who wasn't trying to flirt with her. He didn't stare at her like a creep while they spoke. He kept his eyes on her but in a respectful, paying attention to what you say kind of way. And he didn't dismiss her as just a pretty princess the way many others had.

That night when Regina came to see her, she found Scarlet humming to herself as she was reading through her correspondence from the day. It was the first time since Isabella that Scarlet seemed content; if not happy. It gave her hope that she might finally be starting to heal.

Regina didn't say anything to Scarlet as she took her place at her own desk. Technically Regina was still the Queen. She shared her duties with Scarlet, though, and over the years she had given her more and more responsibility. Now that she finally seemed to be showing signs of healing, Regina thought that perhaps it was time to think of stepping down and making Scarlet the Queen.

Chapter Twenty Seven

John was completely captivated by Scarlet.
He had heard of her beauty, of course. He didn't
think there was anyone in the realm who hadn't heard
about how beautiful she was. He had also heard that
she had had many suitors over the years.

When John came to Wonderland he had no
intention of trying for her hand. He came just to learn.
He hoped to one day be appointed an advisor to the
King in his realm. He had heard the political classes in
Wonderland were the best in all the realms so he made
arrangements to go there.

He found the classes to be imaginative and
insightful. In Regina's class especially they learned to
think outside the box when looking at a problem. She
explained to them that if they enacted protocols and
then only lived by those protocols they missed out on
the chance for growth. While traditions were

necessary it was also necessary to not get stuck in stagnant practices.

He had seen Scarlet around the campus but wasn't in her class. So he was surprised by the invitation to join her to discuss his paper. Then he was even more surprised to find that when it came to ruling she was brilliant. He had been disappointed when they had to end the conversation. But he was hopeful with the invitation to return.

Several days passed before they were able to meet again. In that time he put together a list of books for her to read that had nothing to do with politics and ruling.

At the top of the list was his favorite fantasy book. He also listed some of the basic fairy tale books from his realm, a history book from a realm that was prone to have civil wars, and a comedy book about a couple who were so ridiculously mismatched that their relationship was a miracle to survive all it did.

When they were able to meet again she laughed when he gave her the list. He felt his stomach turn to a ball of knots and his face burn with embarrassment. He was going to make an excuse to leave until she handed him a list that she had created for him. She smiled a brilliant smile at him and they laughed together over the fact they had had the same thought.

Again they sat and talked for hours. Their conversation was much more than politics this time. She told him tales of the history of Wonderland and he shared the history of his realm with her. His stories were pretty basic as his realm was non-magical. Her stories were pretty fantastical because they included the crazy escapades of magical creatures.

Regina passed by the room where they were talking and heard Scarlet genuinely laughing. She felt a fresh surge of hope that Scarlet was finally healing. She went on her way to find the First Elf and get his opinion.

John felt that he could easily fall for Scarlet if he let himself. She was so much more than just beautiful. She was incredibly intelligent and very kind. He sat in on one of her open sessions so he could observe how she dealt with her subjects. He found her to be more than fair. In fact, in a couple of cases he felt that she was much too lenient.

There was one case where a man had been caught red handed having stolen his neighbor's daughter and married her in secret and against her will. Her father insisted that she be returned to him and that the scoundrel must pay a sum to him. Her father had made arrangements for her to marry a rich lord from another realm. He insisted that now her life was ruined as no one else would have her.

Scarlet had the scoundrel pay the fee. She then offered to the father to keep the girl as a worker in the castle and find a suitable husband for her. The father accepted and left the castle a happy man. John felt that the scoundrel should have been treated more harshly than just paying a fine. One look at the girl's tear stained face and he could see her life had been ruined.

Once the father was gone from the castle, Scarlet called the scoundrel forward and gave him his money back. Then she gave him another payment and thanked him for his services. John was about to ask her what she could possibly mean by paying the scoundrel for his crime when the girl started giggling.

Scarlet called her up to where she was sitting and hugged her. She whispered something in her ear and handed her a small bag of money. The girl then left the castle with the scoundrel.

John was sure he had missed something. Upon seeing the extremely confused look on his face, Scarlet let out a little giggle. She then explained to him that the girl had come to her the month before. Her father was going to sell her off to a rich lord who was twice her age and ugly inside and out. She assured her that if it had just been his looks she would have done what she was told but this man had a violent temper and archaic beliefs about women.

Scarlet had brought in a friend from a far off realm. He pretended to be a scoundrel and steal the girl. He then held a not-so-secret wedding ceremony officiated by a fake priest he had brought from his realm. He then took her to a "secret" place; making sure everyone knew where they were going. Now that she was free of her father he was going to take her back to his realm where she could start her life over and live the way she wanted.

John looked at her like she was crazy and asked her if she took that much interest in all her subjects. She told him that as much as she would like to do that , no, she didn't. This girl had been one of her most promising students and she knew that given the chance she would do great things.

After that he realized that she was so much more than a ruler. She was compassionate and really cared about what her people wanted and needed. He knew from that moment that he was in love with her.

Chapter Twenty Eight

Scarlet liked John. A lot. She could feel that their relationship was building to more than just friendship and she wasn't sure what to do. On one hand it was nice to feel happy again. On the other hand she still hadn't given up hope that Isabella was still alive.

She decided to go talk to the First Elf. She hoped he would be able to give her some advice about what to do. She found him in the heart of Wonderland with the Wonderland Tree. He had been waiting for her to seek him out.

He gave her two books. One was a small journal and the other was a large, leather bound tome. He wouldn't tell her what they were or why they were important. He just insisted that she read them and then he disappeared into the trees.

She took the books back to her room to read them. She started with the journal. When she opened it she was surprised to see Isabella's handwriting. Her eyes welled up with tears and she had to wait for them to clear before she could read. What she read didn't make her feel any better.

The journal was about her first love; the one she lost. It went through their entire relationship and ended just before she came to the castle to confront Regina; the day she met Scarlet. Scarlet read through the years of anger and tortured depression she suffered. Scarlet couldn't help but wonder how she could have pushed all of that away when she met her even with the assurances from her beloved about the Scarlet Rose.

Scarlet knew that she herself was nothing like that. Then again, Alex was dead and Alice had gone through the portal with Isabella. There was no one left for her to seek revenge on. The journal did serve as a reminder, though, that Isabella had moved on from her first love.

The tome was interesting. It was a history of battles from across the realms that had been fought because of someone's need for revenge. Out of all of the histories, only two went on to become horrible rulers and were overthrown within months. Of all the ones that were defeated in battle, most of them went on to turn their lives around and move on.

Reading through the two books, Scarlet felt that this was the First Elf's way of telling her it was okay to move on. She took the second book as a warning. Usually the First Elf had a bit of precognition. Oftentimes he could see if something big was coming; just not the particulars. She couldn't help but wonder if he was trying to tell her Alice wasn't as gone as they believed. And if that was the case, how could he be telling her it was okay to move on from Isabella? Was he trying to tell her that she was dead?

Chapter Twenty Nine

Scarlet felt distracted and on edge. How could she follow her heart and allow herself to be happy with John when she didn't fully understand what the First Elf was warning her of? Was Alice still alive and plotting revenge? Did Alice have a friend somewhere in Wonderland that had been biding her time and making plans? She was going to have to talk to the First Elf. She just hoped he actually talked to her this time instead of confusing her more.

She went out to the Wonderland Tree and climbed into its branches as she had when she was a child. She sat looking out at the forest and hoping he would come to her. As she was looking around she noticed a strange flower blooming in the tree. She climbed higher until she could climb along the branch where the flower was.

It was unlike anything she had ever seen before. Its petals were made up of many shades of pink and purple together. It was almost like every petal had been filled in with tiny dots of color all blending together to created a beautiful effect. She leaned down to smell its fragrance and it was like sunshine and chocolate and the scent of a million wildflowers all rolled into one. It was truly the most incredible thing she had ever smelled.

After inhaling the scent, though, she started to feel like she was going to fall asleep. She wanted to crawl back out of the tree before she could fall. Instead, the branch seemed to widen until she was comfortably cocooned. Her eyes drifted closed and she fell into a dream.

In her dream she was consumed with a need to know if Alice and Isabella had survived. She turned away from all of her duties to the realm to follow her obsession. John moved on and left her to it so she was utterly alone. She followed ridiculous leads that led her to many different realms. She was gone from

Wonderland for many years chasing her obsession. When she finally returned to Wonderland it was to find that nearly everything had been destroyed. Both of her parents were dead and the land was suffering. When she finally found a survivor to tell her what had happened they told her that Alice had come soon after she left and waged a war. Without the Scarlet Rose there to protect them they were lost.

Scarlet woke from her dream in a panic. It had all seemed so real that she could taste the decay of the land on her tongue still. She looked around frantically to reassure herself that it had really only been a dream and came face to face with the First Elf.

He assured her that it had only been a dream; however it was a dream with a kernel of truth. He did not know if either Alice or Isabella had survived. They should not have as they had gone through a portal to nowhere. However, they were both creatures of magic and it was possible their magic created a new land much as the Estrella had created Wonderland.

Thinking it over Scarlet thought it was unlikely that Isabella had survived. Surely in all that time she would have found a way back to her if she had. Scarlet also wasn't convinced that a new land had been created from their magic. If it had she would have heard about it. She had contacts in every known realm.

They pondered the possibilities together for quite a while. Neither one of them wanted to definitely rule anything out. After all, nothing was ever as concrete as it seemed; especially when it came to magic. She was ready to go back to the castle when he broached the idea with her of the possibility of her taking over as Queen. The idea actually startled her.

The combination of Wonderland magic and her own magic had made Regina immortal when she came to Wonderland. There was no reason for her to ever step aside as the Queen. Scarlet had never even considered there may come a day when Regina didn't want to be the Queen.

As she considered the possibility, she realized that she was ready. She was already partially ruling. She met with her subjects regularly and knew the people and the land. She had friends in every realm she could call on if needed. And most importantly, she had mastered her magic. Not only that but her magic was stronger than Regina's. There really was nothing left to hold her back from taking over if that was what Regina wanted.

So she agreed to talk it over with Regina. But there was something else she wanted to do first.

Chapter Thirty

John was in his room trying to read. Emphasis on trying. He wasn't having much luck with his studies because he was thinking about Scarlet.

He lived in constant anticipation of their conversations. She was incredible. He could talk to her for hours and never run out of things to say. He was amazed by her intellect and by her beauty. Every time he closed his eyes he could see her face. Every night in his dreams he saw her face. He desperately wanted more of a relationship with her but he was afraid to push her.

John didn't know much about Isabella. He knew the basic history; the battle, the portal, the search. He didn't know that Scarlet and Isabella had been a couple though. They had been very private and few people in Wonderland knew the truth. They all believed that they had merely been close friends. He was about to learn, though.

The knock at his door startled him. When he saw Scarlet standing there he couldn't help the smile that spread across his face. He let her in and as soon as they were both seated she began to talk.

She started from the first time she met Isabella to the day she went through the portal. John just stared at her as she went through this information overload. When she finished he took her hand. He looked her in the eyes and thanked her for sharing her story with him.

Still looking in her eyes he assured her that he was there for her no matter what. If she just wanted to be friends that would be okay. If she wanted more that was okay too. He would go at whatever pace she wanted to go. He wanted to make sure she understood that her friendship meant everything to him.

She had tears rolling down her face as he finished giving her his assurances. She leaned in and kissed him softly, gave a whispered thanks, then left the room. He sat and started at the door after she left. His mind was reeling.

He could tell from their conversations that there had been love in her past but he had never guessed at any of this. He hadn't lied to her. He cherished her friendship. And he truly believed the past was the past. He just really hoped this was the first step toward a future.

The next time he saw her she acted very shy and like she wasn't at all sure of him. He was sure that she felt uncomfortable and like maybe she had shared too much. He was careful to act normal around her. He kept the conversation going the way it always did until he could tell she was comfortable. After that he let her lead the conversation.

Over the course of the next couple of weeks he could tell that she became more comfortable. Their relationship progressed naturally. He had never been happier and he could tell she was happy too. He just hoped it was really him making her happy and not just her desire to prove to herself that she could be.

Chapter Thirty One

Scarlet had felt immensely relieved after she told John her history. His reaction had made her want to cry with how sweet it was. After she left his room, though, she had doubts. It was easy for him to be comforting and generous right after the fact. But what about after he'd had time to process?

So the next time she saw him she was nervous and shy. Once she realized he was acting exactly the same as he always had she was able to relax. It didn't take long after that before she fell in love.

Their first real kiss was magical. They were out in the gardens and the flowers were singing quietly to them. They strolled through the gardens hand in hand without a word; just enjoying being together and the warmth of the day. They came to a bench under an apple tree. The tree was in bloom and looked and smelled magnificent.

They sat together on the bench. He was looking at her like she was the most beautiful thing he'd ever seen. Without even really thinking about what she was doing, she leaned in and kissed him. It was a soft, sweet kiss that deepened until they both had to pull back and take a breath.

When they pulled back he smiled at her and his smile was kind of shy. She thought to herself that she was one lucky woman to have this man in her life.

Scarlet had approached Regina a few days after her talk with John about her past. They sat down and discussed what it would mean for both of them for Scarlet to become Queen. When first thinking about it Scarlet hadn't really considered how much would actually change. In her mind she saw the coronation and title change and that was all. Regina had other plans.

Regina wanted to travel the realms. She had made trips here and there but they were never long and she always had to return to Wonderland within a month. The magic here was what kept her alive. The First Elf had now found a way for her to do the traveling she wanted without dying.

This meant that once Scarlet took the crown she would also be taking on all the responsibilities that they currently shared. Scarlet would have to cut back on teaching. There would be a lot more for her to do around the castle. It was all doable. She just wasn't sure if she was ready for all of that responsibility.

She asked Regina to give her a week to think it all through. She didn't just spend the week thinking, though. She sat down with John and went through everything. Every way her life would change. Every responsibility she would have to take on. Every way it would affect Wonderland.

She looked at every possible scenario and worked out the ways to handle it all. By the end of the week she agreed that she was ready to step up and take the responsibility. She told John she just had one thing she wanted to do before she took the crown. She looked at him with hope in her eyes as she told him she wanted to get married.

Chapter Thirty Two

It only took a week to get everything in place for the perfect "fairytale" wedding. Scarlet was amazed at how many of her friends from different realms were able to come on such short notice. John didn't have any family or even friends from his realm.

He stood at the front of the aisle watching as Scarlet walked toward him. He felt his face would split open from the grin he wore. He had never been this happy before.

When they said their vows everyone cheered. When they shared their kiss they were suddenly enveloped in a bright ball of light. He could feel energy coursing through him that was unlike anything he had ever felt before. When they parted he heard a gasp from the crowd. He looked down at himself and saw his body was glowing faintly. When he looked up at Scarlet he saw the same glow emitting from her.

He felt different. More than just happy; he felt a pulse of life flowing through him. He reached out a hand to touch Scarlet and when their hands connected it sent a pulse of energy through the surrounding area.

Suddenly the ground beneath their feet began to tremble. They jumped back together, still holding hands, just as something began to sprout from the ground where they had been standing. Everyone watched in awe as a tree sprouted up and grew to full maturity.

It was incredibly beautiful. Its leaves were shimmering gold and silver. It had tiny, delicate pink flowers interspersed with large, robust blue flowers. The difference between the two was striking but the way they blended together made the overall effect stunning.

The First Elf came forward and held up a hand to get everyone's attention. He had seen this phenomenon once before. This was a True Love Tree. When two types of magic are combined by true love it can create a living tree. This tree is not only a testament to the love that created it but also had a magic of its own. Like the Wonderland Tree, this tree had the ability to create life, heal wounds, and keep the realm alive. This tree would bring change and new life into Wonderland.

John was staring at him in shock. He insisted over and over that he didn't have any kind of magic. Once he was calm enough to hear what others were saying the First Elf explained that he had always sensed something magical about him but that magic had been dormant until they had shared true love's kiss. Scarlet's magic was extremely powerful. That, combined with his emotional state and the kiss, had been enough to awaken his magic.

He looked over at Scarlet who was beaming at him. He gave a "it doesn't matter" shrug and pulled her into his arms. This time when they kissed the large blue flowers opened up and released thousands of butterflies. They were every color imaginable and created the illusion that a cloud of rainbows was floating above them. Everyone applauded and the reception officially began.

The party was the most lavish event Wonderland had ever seen. It lasted all through the night and well into the next morning. There was an abundance of food. Scarlet and Regina had worked together to make "fairy drinks" that allowed their guests to sprout wings for about an hour. There was music and dancing. It was the most wonderful night of John's life and, judging by her smile, Scarlet's too.

When the party ended they headed off on their honeymoon. Scarlet had planned this as a surprise to him. Deep in the woods of Wonderland, Scarlet had found a cottage that had been built inside a large, hollowed out tree. It was obvious it had been done with magic but the craftsmanship was still incredible.

Inside the cottage there was a room filled with books about magic that she had never seen before. There were also books about plants, creatures, architecture, and history. It was obvious from the dust that this cottage had been abandoned for a long time. Scarlet had asked the First Elf if he knew who it had belonged to and he had told her that it had been Isabella's.

Regina had tried to talk Scarlet out of taking John there. She thought it was insensitive; almost like Scarlet was telling him he was nothing more than what she was settling for. But something inside Scarlet insisted that she needed to take him there. That there was something there that they needed to find together.

They spent the first night there in each other's arms. They took the time to really explore and get to know each other on an intimate level. The next day they began their exploration of the cottage.

Scarlet worried that exploring the place where Isabella had lived would depress her but really it had the opposite effect. She was fascinated as she looked through things that were a part of Isabella before she knew her. There was so much about her that Scarlet had never known. On top of that the books of magic were full of things Scarlet never knew existed.

While she was poring over one of these books John found a loose floorboard that he decided to explore. In the space underneath it he found a jewelry box. Inside the box was a small locket. It was an oval shape with a rose bud etched into the top of it. When he opened the locket he found a small purple gem nestled inside it.

He reached in with two fingers to pick up the gem. As soon as he touched it, his whole body began to glow. His eyes glazed over and his face went slack.

Scarlet came running over to him to see what was happening. She reached out to take his hands and his eyes focused on her.

The glow faded from his body but his whole face lit up like it was Christmas morning. When he finally found his voice, he shocked Scarlet into a stunned disbelief with what he had to say.

Chapter Thirty Three

When Isabella and Alice went through the portal they could feel the nothingness sucking them in. They clung to each other and through sheer force of will they managed to open a new portal within the portal. The force of the two portals warring with each other wreaked havoc on them both.

When they were finally deposited into an actual realm they had both been irrevocably altered. Alice now resembled the little girl she had pretended to be when she first met the Hatter. She still had her memories but no magic. She looked around for Isabella and instead found a young boy standing with her.

Somehow the magic of the warring portals had completely changed Isabella into a little boy. It had also gave her false memories. She truly believed she was a little orphan boy born in this realm. She had memories of an orphanage that she lived at. She even had memories of the people.

Alice let her lead her into the village to see just how far this magic went. She was completely surprised that the villagers knew the boy. This magic ran deep. With Isabella so completely altered by this magic she knew she didn't have to worry about her.

She let herself be taken in by the orphanage so at least she would be cared for while she tried to figure out how to get her magic back and how to get back to Wonderland. After a few days there, though, she was taken in by a wealthy villager.

Isabella, or John as she was known here, stayed at the orphanage. He studied hard and the teachers at the village school noticed. They took the time to work with him so that when he was old enough he could go to the University in Wonderland. Alice's time in his life had been so brief that he forgot all about her before he ever got to Wonderland.

The magic that had created this whole illusion for him was broken by the gem but not fully. Isabella had been storing parts of her magic in the gem in the years between her lover's death until the day she met Scarlet. When she met Scarlet she had left everything behind.

The magic from the gem didn't change everything. Her body remained a man's body but she had her memories back. Including the fact that Alice was still alive.

Chapter Thirty Four

Alice remained with the wealthy villager until she grew into womanhood. She was considered to be a great beauty by everyone in the village. So much so that the youngest prince of the realm, a young man who was only a few years older than herself (or at least as old as she appeared to be) was seeking her hand in marriage.

She allowed him to court her but only as a means to an end. Being in his good graces meant she spent a lot of time at the palace. While there she was able to hear the gossip of the other realms. She had gotten very good at leading conversations to discussions of Wonderland.

During the year that the Prince courted her, she learned a lot about everything that had gone on in Wonderland since the day she went through the portal. When she learned of Scarlet's impending marriage, to be followed in a month by her coronation, she knew she would need to act soon. Regina and her daughter would be too busy with these happy affairs to prepare for an attack.

The problem was she had no way to attack them. She lost all of her magic when she went through the portals. She believed that the reason that happened was because the portals were somehow trying to protect Isabella. They had changed everything about her and made her as non-threatening as possible. It was like the portal took all of her glamour magic and used it on Isabella.

Alice realized all of this after the fact though. By the time she went looking for the boy she couldn't remember anything about him.

Of course, that could have been the magic at play, still trying to protect him. When she asked about him at the orphanage no one there could remember him even though he had lived there for fifteen years.

She thought her best bet would be to travel to Wonderland and see if just being back in the realm restored her magic. She wasn't sure how to go about making the trip, though. As the possible future Princess she was too well guarded to go alone. Her best bet would be to get the Prince to take her to Scarlet's royal wedding; assuming, of course, he was even invited.

The wedding was only two days away so she decided to just ask him if they were going. He told her his family had been invited and while his parents were gong he wasn't sure he wanted to. She did her best flirtatious manipulation to talk him into it and the next day they were on their way to Wonderland.

As they crossed the border into Wonderland she held her breath and waited to see if she felt anything. She almost burst into tears when she felt nothing. She had to keep control of herself while she was with the royal family, though. Once she was alone she tried a few of the minor spells she had always been able to do and nothing worked.

She was angry and frustrated but she was far from ready to give up. Wonderland was full of magic. There had to be some way to steal it from somewhere. If she could just recharge then maybe she could have full power again. Then she would be able to get her revenge and take over the realm. She needed help but she doubted she would find any here. People were too happy under the current ruler.

Later that evening there was a knock at her door. When she answered it she was shocked to see the First Elf standing there. So far no one else had recognized her. There had been a couple of workers at the Inn they were staying at who had said she resembled the storybook pictures of Alice but that was it.

The First Elf had instructed all the workers at every Inn as well as everyone in the castle to be on the lookout. If they saw anyone who looked like Alice used to then they were to report it to him. He was surprised, though, to find it wasn't a glamour. Not only that but she had no magic at all.

Alice glowered at him as he mused aloud about this interesting turn of events. Before she could say anything, though, he told her there was no way for her to steal magic. The part of her that had housed magic within her was now gone and without that she had no way of harnessing any.

Sitting through the ceremony the next day she was as awed as everyone as the True Love Tree sprouted. She couldn't think of any way to use it to her advantage, though, because it grew out of their magic. Besides, it wasn't like she could dig it up and take it back with her. And she knew now she was going to have to go back. If she stayed in Wonderland her every move would be watched by that blasted Elf.

She would go back and continue her courtship with the Prince. If she were to marry him she would have royal standing. That would give her an excuse to go back to Wonderland whenever she wanted. She was going to have to give that some serious consideration.

The ride back with the Prince and his family was loud. They were all going on and on about the True Love Tree. They didn't really talk about anything new. It was a phenomenon that none of them had ever seen before or were likely to ever see again. It was likely that they were going to be talking about this for a long time.

Alice decided she could use this distraction as a way to do some research. There was a wizard living in the realm. She was able to visit with him on the pretense of learning about herbs and medicines. They were alone during their lessons so she felt comfortable throwing in questions about magic.

After a couple of weeks of this he put up a hand to stop her mid question. He told her he knew who she was and what she really wanted. He told her the same thing the First Elf had. There was no way for her to get her magic back. He was willing to help her get her revenge by using magic, though.

Chapter Thirty Five

The magician had tried to study in Wonderland. He had only been there for about a month before he was asked to leave. They had disapproved of his way of using magic and said it was too dark. He did have a morbid fascination with what others considered dark magic but he would never hurt anyone. He really had a very gentle soul.

Being asked to leave Wonderland had hardened him a bit. Not enough to want to kill anyone, but enough to agree to help Alice remove them from power. He just didn't realize how deep Alice's thirst for revenge really went.

As a boy the Magician, Theodore, had learned early on what his powers could do. He loved to heal hurt animals and help plants grow. But he also had a fascination with death. He would study dead things he found. He had learned many uses for death in spells and even in medicines. But he never killed for this. He only used what he found.

His professor in Wonderland, not Scarlet, had found this to be distasteful and used it as grounds to expel him from the school. He had gone back to his own realm and continued with his experiments. Then Alice entered his life.

He had read the legends when he was in Wonderland and recognized her from the pictures. At first he thought she was just a doppelganger but when she started with the leading questions he realized pretty quickly what her true identity was. He agreed to help her because he felt that if Scarlet were not in charge he may not have been forced out. He didn't know that not only did Scarlet have nothing to do with it, but she didn't know anything about it.

The professor had learned that Theo was a descendent of Maleficent. He was terrified of her and her ability to transform into a dragon. The professor didn't know if Theo had the ability or not but he wasn't going to take a chance to find out. He used his work with dead things as an excuse to ask him to leave. He never told Scarlet any of it because Regina had once been friends with Maleficent and would have wanted the boy to stay.

Theo and Alice worked up a plan together. Or, at least, Alice worked up a plan and told Theo just enough to make him comfortable. Alice's idea was to burn down the Wonderland Tree. Without the tree Wonderland would die. What she told Theo was that he would set the tree on fire which would bring Scarlet out to defend it; giving him a chance to defeat her.

Alice realized early on that while Theo wanted revenge he had a very strong sense of morality. He wanted to depose Scarlet and Regina but didn't want to hurt them. Alice pretended to feel the same way in order to lead him along. Theo believed in the good in people and took Alice at her word.

Theo used his magic to disguise both of them and they snuck out of the realm at night. They made their way to the edge of the realm and once they were sure they weren't followed they portalled into Wonderland.

They camped out in the woods that night. At first light they made their way through the woods to the Wonderland Tree. Theo would need some time to prepare. He intended to set a magical fire that wouldn't actually hurt the tree. He didn't know that Alice had replaced some of his ingredients so that the fire would be real.

Theo got everything put together and was ready to go. Before he could put his spell into action, though, Scarlet stepped in front of him. Regina and the First Elf were with her. She didn't say anything to him. In fact, it was like she didn't see him there at all. She focused her attention solely on Alice.

The more she ignored him, the angrier Theo got. He could feel his anger building inside him. He felt like his blood was beginning to boil and his skin began to itch. He didn't know what was happening to him but he was too angry to care. Before he knew it he was transforming. Everyone stared in shock as he turned into a giant dragon.

He was beautiful. His scales were a blending of shades of black and grey with some purple spread throughout. Anywhere the sun hit his scales he sparkled like there were a million flecks of glitter in them.

He reared back and let loose a stream of fire aimed directly at the tree. Scarlet jumped in front of it and threw up a protective spell. Once he stopped spouting the fire she counter-attacked. She was just trying to push him back away from the tree but he saw it as her trying to hurt him. He continued to try to burn the tree and she continued to try to push him back.

As their magic crashed into each other's over and over again it sent sparks flying up into the air over their heads. A cloud began to form and build quickly. It wasn't long before it was crackling and ready to burst.

A bolt of lightning shot out of the cloud and directly at the Wonderland Tree. With an angry crack the tree split down the middle. The earth beneath their feet shuddered. Scarlet immediately turned her back on Theo and rushed to the tree.

Chapter Thirty Six

Seeing Scarlet turn her back on him to rush to the tree took all of the fight out of Theo. He shifted back to his human form and went to help her. She was on her knees in front of the tree whispering healing words of magic.

Before he could get to Scarlet he saw Alice heading toward her. He knew Alice couldn't help because she had no magic. He saw the knife in her hand and only just managed to shield Scarlet before Alice plunged it down toward her. He turned his magic on Alice and cocooned her in magic. It kept her stuck in place.

Once she was secure, he went to help Scarlet. Regina and the First Elf had already joined her and were lending their magic to help. Before he joined them he asked the nearby talking flowers to get the word out that they needed help. Then he leaned down to help the others as they whispered healing words of magic to the tree.

The effects of the damaged tree could be felt all over Wonderland. The talking flowers were losing their ability to talk. There were tremors running under the ground throughout the land. Trees were being uprooted. Wonderland was dying.

The word spread quickly, though. Scarlet's widespread friendships were soon evident as magic users from every realm were portaling into Wonderland to help.

Very slowly the tree began to mend. Little by little the combined magic of hundreds of magic users working together began to knit the tree back together. As the magic was working Scarlet stood and took off the Scarlet Rose from where she wore it around her neck. She reached in and placed it in the center of the rift then watched as the magic fused the tree around it.

When the last bit of the tree had mended together a pulse of pure magic shot out of it and into the land. Everyone watched incredulously as the tree pulled itself up from the ground and began to walk away. Scarlet quickly began to follow it and then everyone else began to follow. The tree made its way slowly and carefully through the woods. It was being extra careful not to hurt any of the other trees or plants in its path.

Once out of the woods it picked up the pace a little while still being careful of its surroundings. It made its way across the land to where the True Love Tree stood.

Everyone watched in awe as the Wonderland Tree crashed into the True Love Tree. Scarlet went to rush forward but John grabbed her arm and pulled her back. The two trees seemed to be melding into each other. Before long the two trees stood together as one.

The remaining tree was magnificent. The bark looked like each small piece was made of silver and gold. The leaves were large and the way the silver and gold intertwined on them made them sparkle with a dazzling intensity. The pink and blue flowers had merged together into huge purple flowers. Overall the sight was stunning.

As they all stood staring at the tree's magnificence, reports began to be brought to Scarlet from all over Wonderland. Everything was more alive. The colors were more vibrant. Anyone who had even the smallest spark of magic before was able to perform much more magic than they ever could before.

Scarlet herself felt different. She felt stronger. She turned to look at John and saw that he was completely changed. He was still a man but he looked more feminine. He looked a lot more like Isabella now. In fact, Scarlet could see Isabella in his eyes.

They took Alice back to the castle and locked her in a tower room. Scarlet refused to put her in the dungeon. After all, she didn't have any magic that could help her escape. On top of that, her reason for wanting revenge was valid in Scarlet's eyes. Alice had lost her love.

Scarlet hoped that by not treating Alice as a prisoner that they could rehabilitate her. That maybe someday she would move on with her life and find something new to live for.

Chapter Thirty Seven

Scarlet, John, Regina, the First Elf, and even Theo, who had stayed on in Wonderland as an advisor, took turns visiting with Alice.

Scarlet brought her the tome on revenge stories that the First Elf had brought her. She came and visited with her a couple of times a week. She told her stories of her childhood. Shared the stories of other realms. She hoped she was painting a picture for her of what a big world it was and how much possibility there was for happiness.

Regina shared stories of Alex, the Hatter, from when he first came to Wonderland. She told her of his hats and his mannerisms. She also told her of the deal they had made and how Alex would never have been able to have children. Alice flew into a rage at this. She had wasted all that time with a man who would never give her children once he had gotten all of the running around out of his system. She had never known that.

When Theo visited with her they studied together. He was teaching her the history of the different realms. They also read together from what was considered the great literature of different realms. He felt that she was growing as a person. He had even greater hope for her future than Scarlet did.

The years passed with Alice being kept a prisoner. As time passed she was given some freedoms. She was allowed out of her room and into the grounds as long as she had guards with her. She was invited to dine with the family instead of in her room.

Scarlet watched her closely as the years passed. She saw the changes in her as they came about. She lost the look of hatred in her eyes whenever she looked at Regina and Scarlet. She began to interact with others. After about three years had passed, Scarlet decided to give Alice a job.

Scarlet took Alice over to the school. Scarlet had noticed that she seemed to have an affinity towards children. What Scarlet did was set up a class for young children who were just beginning to learn to read. She set Alice up as their teacher with a friend of Theo's as her assistant. The friend was to report back to Scarlet on Alice's progress.

Over the course of a year Scarlet stopped by the class a few times. She was impressed by Alice's way with the children. They were advancing so quickly under her tutelage that they all seemed years older than they were. The assistant assured Scarlet that there was nothing at all magical about their level of learning. Alice was simply very patient and very good at her job.

It was shortly after that visit that Scarlet moved Alice out of the castle. She had a cottage built for her close to the school. They all still spent time with her though. Scarlet had come to think of her as a friend and she really hoped Alice felt the same way.

There was peace in the realm and everyone was happy. That is until the morning they woke to find Alice was gone and the Scarlet Rose had been dug out of the Wonderland Tree.

Part Three

It all started with Alice. Now, thanks to her, Wonderland was in turmoil. Everything was floundering. Peace was nothing more than a wishful dream. Scarlet was going to find Alice. Find her and end it once and for all.

Chapter Thirty Eight

It was a few days after Scarlet announced her pregnancy when Alice disappeared. Alice had not seemed to be happy about the news. But Scarlet never thought she would do something like this.

Wonderland wasn't dying; not like it had been before. But it was no longer flourishing, either. It was like a blanket of weariness settled over the land. Scarlet could feel it but refused to give in to it. She had her unborn child to think about.

Her pregnancy went remarkably well considering the turmoil in the land. Scarlet continued to teach. She continued to meet with the people of the realm and hear their concerns and suggestions. At night she would visit the Wonderland Tree long after the realm was asleep. She would place both of her hands on the trunk and whisper words of healing magic.

After she left the tree the First Elf would come out and whisper healing magic to it as well. Sometimes Regina would join him. During the day Theo whispered to the tree as well. They were all doing their part. In this way they kept Wonderland going.

The day Scarlet gave birth was the first day that Wonderland really started to heal. She insisted on being outside and under the Wonderland Tree. She wasn't sure how she knew but she somehow knew that giving birth under the tree would be what it needed to heal.

She gave birth to a beautiful baby boy. He had her bright red hair but his eyes were a lighter green. He had a birthmark just under his cheek in the shape of a key.

People came from all over to see the little Prince. Regina worried that the birth would bring Alice back for revenge. Scarlet believed that Alice had nothing to do with the theft of the Scarlet Rose. She believed that whoever had done it had taken Alice too so that it would look like she was responsible. She held firm to that belief when everyone else tried to talk her out of it.

Everyone also tried to talk her out of throwing a party to celebrate the birth of the baby. She thought it was actually pretty funny that Theo kept reminding her of his great-grandmother's legacy.

The party went off without a hitch. She and John announced to everyone the baby's name. They had decided to name him Nicholas.

The whole of Wonderland came out for the party. So did all of Scarlet's friends from other realms. Everyone was on the lookout for Alice but there was no sign of her. The party ended with no issues and Nicholas was put to bed.

Scarlet tried again to convince everyone that Alice was a victim and not the one they should be fearing. No one seemed willing to listen. Even John wasn't buying it. But she was sticking to her belief.

Chapter Thirty Nine

Nicholas had a great childhood. Very early on he showed signs of magical ability. Regina, Scarlet, and the First Elf all worked with him. He was also an incredibly kind child. He was nice to everyone. It reminded Scarlet of how the Wonderland Tree had been so careful on its way through Wonderland to the True Love Tree.

Nicholas' favorite place was the Wonderland Tree. Every chance he got he would sneak off to be there. It got to the point where they started holding his lessons there. He seemed to have some kind of bond with the tree that no one understood. It was almost like the tree talked to him.

When Nicholas turned five he insisted that he needed to spend the night sleeping in the tree. He refused to be talked out of it. John was completely against it. Scarlet was considering it but was understandably nervous. It was the First Elf who swayed them both.

The First Elf had been watching Nicholas' relationship with the tree. He believed that the sentient part of the tree had bonded with Nicholas when he was born beneath it. Nicholas could hear the tree in a way no one else could. This relationship was what was healing Wonderland. He had somehow replaced the Scarlet Rose.

With the First Elf's belief that Nicholas' relationship with the tree was so important to Wonderland, Scarlet and John agreed to let him spend the night in the tree.

There were no obvious changes in Nicholas the next morning but there were some in the tree. The purple flowers had turned red. Where the bark had been silver and gold before it was now more of an onyx color. The leaves were still a blend of silver and gold but they were even bigger than they had been before.

The overall effect was stunning but they worried a little about the new darkness of the bark. Some took it as a bad omen.

Scarlet ran her hands over the bark and found it was much harder now. She thought the darkness was more of a defense mechanism. She just hoped that it wasn't a sign that bad things were coming to Wonderland. She could almost feel everyone's fears seeping into her.

When a year had passed and nothing had happened everyone began to relax a little. As they approached Nicholas's sixth birthday he made it clear that he would be sleeping in the Wonderland Tree again. This time the changes in the tree were much less noticeable. The red flowers were bigger. The leaves seemed a little shiner. That was it.

As each year passed, Nicholas would spend the night of his birthday sleeping in the Wonderland Tree. Each year there would be subtle differences in the tree in the morning. It wasn't until Nicholas turned ten that there was any noticeable change to his person.

When he climbed down from the tree the morning after his tenth birthday Scarlet gasped. Where his eyes had been a nice shade of green before one was silver and the other was gold. He also had a much stronger sense of magic radiating off him. The tree on the other hand, showed no changes that year.

Scarlet worried that there would be changes to Nicholas' personality. It took her a few months to let go of that fear. Nicholas was delighted by the change in his eye color. He was still kind to everyone he met. He was still devoted to his studies.

It was about six months after his tenth birthday that Scarlet went to wake Nicholas and found his room empty. Her first thought was that he had risen early and gone to the tree. There had been many mornings when she had to hunt him down there.

She took her time getting to the tree as it was beautiful weather out. She was enjoying the feel of the warm sunshine on her face. When she got to the tree she found Nicholas' bag but no Nicholas. She scanned the tree to see if he was up in the branches but saw no sign of him. She raced around the tree to see if he was hiding on the other side but he wasn't there either.

Instead she found the First Elf. He was laying sprawled on the ground. For the first time in Scarlet's long life he looked like a frail old man. She dropped to the ground next to him and could feel that he had no magic left in him. His eyes were blind. He looked like the gentlest breeze would blow him away.

Scarlet could feel his life was ebbing away and she had no way to help him. She touched a finger to her wedding ring. She and John had had the rings made with special magic. All they had to do was touch it with their index finger and whisper the word "wonder" and it would let the other know they needed them and guide them on where to go.

The First Elf was trying to speak to her. His words were such a soft whisper that even with her ear right next to his mouth she couldn't tell what he was saying. By the time John got to her the First Elf was dead.

Regina felt the Wonderland Tree shudder. Then without warning it reached out a branch and gently picked up the body. A hole opened in the side of the trunk and the branch carefully placed the body in the hole. The hole closed over the First Elf until all that was left was the impression of this face in the bark.

Scarlet couldn't take the time to dwell on his death, though. Nicholas was missing and she had to find him. She just had no clue where to start looking.

Chapter Forty

Nicholas had gone to the Wonderland Tree in the night. In his dreams he could hear it calling to him. His walk to the tree was practically a dream.

As he got closer he could hear the tree's warning more clearly. It was warning him that danger was coming and he needed to get to the tree for protection. The tree was in sight when arms reached out and grabbed him. He felt a necklace being slipped over his head. When he tried to lash out with his magic nothing happened.

He struggled with all of his strength but whoever was holding him was very strong. He saw the First Elf running toward him and felt a surge of hope. He had no idea how it happened but the person holding him shot a burst of magic at the First Elf without letting go of him. The magic hit the First Elf and he collapsed to the ground.

Nicholas felt a warm sensation against his chest. He looked down to see the Scarlet Rose around his neck. It was absorbing the First Elf's magic.

Once the First Elf was powerless, the arms holding him let go. He wanted to run but his legs wouldn't work. He was in too much shock.

His captor opened a portal then picked him up and carried him through it. He could feel all sensation leaving his body and darkness creeping in. When they were through the portal he saw the outline of a large castle before darkness overtook him and he passed out.

When he woke up he found he was in a bedroom. Looking around he could see no door but there were windows. He went to look out one and saw that he was very high up. He couldn't feel his magic so he knew he couldn't use it to escape.

He looked down and saw the Scarlet Rose still around his neck. When he tried to take it off he received an electrical shock. He quickly let go.

He looked around the room again and decided to explore it. He looked through every drawer of the dresser, under the bed, even under the rug. He found nothing that would help him escape. There was a mirror in a frame sitting on the dresser. He took it down and tried to see if he could use it to get through to someone at home.

He was just about to give up and put it back when a woman appeared in the mirror. She told him that the Scarlet Rose nullified his magic and it would be useless for him to try to escape without magic. She told him his captor had placed a spell on the chain that made it impossible for anyone but her to take it off him.

He asked her why she was holding him captive and she told him that she wasn't the captor. She was a captive herself. She introduced herself as Alice. She was trapped inside the mirror. She has been taken from Wonderland a long time ago.

He asked her to tell him everything she could about their captor. She didn't know much. The captor had been so furious that Alice didn't have magic and wouldn't help her. She had wanted her to give up information on Wonderland and specifically on Scarlet but she wouldn't do it. The captor had trapped her in the mirror in a rage and had left her there ever since.

Nicholas wasn't sure what to make of this development. His mother had always believed in their friendship. She had been so certain that Alice hadn't been the one who stole the Scarlet Rose.

The tree had never seen a face to be able to tell him who did it. Alice didn't know who it was either, other than that it was a woman. Nicholas was just going to have to wait for her to come to him.

Chapter Forty One

Scarlet organized a huge search party. They went from house to house, through every inch of the woods, and every bit of the University. They went over every bit of Wonderland three times over but there was no sign of him anywhere.

Scarlet finally had to admit that Nicholas wasn't anywhere in Wonderland. She contacted every friend she had in every realm and begged them to search their realms for him. Days went by and no one found him. Scarlet went deeper and deeper into depression the longer Nicholas was gone.

Days turned into weeks. Weeks turned into months. Scarlet refused to let her depression keep her from her search. She was almost manic in her search. John was a bit more laid back. He spent time going through the library and searching for anything he could find to try to track him down.

It was Regina who suggested that it could be someone from one of the realms Scarlet visited as a child. She could think of two realms in particular where she had made possible enemies. The first one was the vain King and Queen. Dean, the son who was ruling the realm had searched the realm for Nicholas but hadn't found him. His father had died but the Queen was still there. Regina thought it was possible that grief had changed her perspective on ruling.

The second was the Queen with many children who wanted to use them to take over other realms. Regina had stripped her of her powers but it was possible she had stolen the Scarlet Rose to be able to use its power. Richard had searched his realm but had found nothing.

Scarlet knew from her time with Alex, though, that it was possible to hide people away if you really wanted to. She was going to have to look closer into the two suspects.

Chapter Forty Two

Nicholas lost track of time. He wasn't sure if he had been captive for days or months. His captor brought him food once a day but didn't talk to him. At least, he thought it was his captor. They wore a mask over their face so he had no idea who it really was.

If it wasn't for Alice's company he probably would have gone mad. He had heard all the stories from his parents about the past and Alice. It was kind of nice to hear them from her perspective. He told her some stories of Wonderland but he was very careful about what he said. He had a feeling that the only reason Alice was in the room with him was so their captor could listen to their conversations and use them to learn more about Wonderland.

He explored every nook and cranny of the room. He found nothing there that would help him escape. He also found nothing that would lead him to the identity of his captor. He was frustrated and angry but he never lost hope. He knew that somehow his parents would find him.

At night he dreamed of the Wonderland Tree. He longed to be up in the branches. The tree was more than just a piece of Wonderland history to him. The tree was his friend. When he was with the tree he could hear it. From anywhere in Wonderland he could hear it. He figured he must not be in Wonderland now if couldn't hear his tree.

He would stare out the window every now and then to see if he could learn anything from the surrounding area that would tell him where he was. There was a large lake nearby. He could also see the edge of a forest. He could see people out and about and working the grounds but that didn't tell him much. He was too high up to see their faces. The only indication he saw was that they all had black hair. This told him he was in one of two realms; Richard or Dean.

He knew the two rulers of the "dark haired realms" as his mother had called them. He didn't believe that either Dean or Richard would imprison him though. They were too good of friends with his mother. However, in both of those realms his mother had helped the current rulers rise to power. Maybe the overthrown parents were responsible?

Chapter Forty Three

Scarlet traveled to Richard's realm first. John had found a spell in some of the First Elf's old journals that would allow her to search for magically hidden places. If Nicholas were being held in a secret room like she had been they would be able to find it.

She went without John. He stayed behind to continue reading through the journals. Even if they found a room hidden by magic they had no way of getting in yet. He was searching for the answer to that problem.

She started with Richard because his mother was the most likely one to have taken the Scarlet Rose. She had been stripped of all magic when she was sent through the mirror into Wonderland. It stood to reason she wanted to use the power from the Scarlet Rose to get revenge. Especially since she had been kept a prisoner in Wonderland for ten years before she had been freed and allowed to return to her own realm.

When she had returned she had been set up in a cottage outside of the castle grounds. Richard wanted her where he could keep an eye on her without actually having her in the castle.

They went to the cottage and found it empty. It hadn't been abandoned. She just wasn't there. Scarlet left a note on her table asking that she come up to the castle to meet with her when she returned. They went back to the castle to begin the search for a secret hidden room.

They had been at it for a couple of hours and were almost finished when Richard's mother arrived. She was perfectly polite toward Scarlet even though her eyes were shooting daggers at her. She denied having any knowledge of Nicholas or his whereabouts. She insisted she hadn't been back to Wonderland since her release years ago.

Scarlet didn't believe her but didn't think she was working alone. Her oldest son, who had been sent to Wonderland with her, was still in Wonderland. He had been released from prison after only a year and had stayed there. He was currently enrolled in the University and was a model student. Scarlet didn't think he was helping her.

She portalled to Dean's realm the next morning. His mother had been living in the castle the whole time since Dean had taken over. Her husband had died about six months before the Scarlet Rose had been taken. Dean had seen some changes in his mother but nothing that would make him think she was capable of hurting people like this.

Scarlet did her meeting with the mom before her search of the castle. She found that she was very much changed from when Scarlet had lived there. She was quieter and softer. She wasn't all glamoured up like she used to be. She was quiet and seemed genuinely concerned.

Scarlet didn't believe a word she said. She began to wonder if somehow the two mothers were working together. If they were holding Nicholas somewhere else. There were no signs of him in this castle either.

Chapter Forty Four

Nicholas suddenly felt a flare of warmth come from the Scarlet Rose. He hadn't been trying to take it off. He hadn't been trying to do anything. He wandered over to the window to think. As he sat there looking out he saw his mother walk toward the lake and open a portal.

He wondered if the flare of warmth was the Scarlet Rose keeping him hidden. He knew the story of Alex and the secret room. He figured his mother would have found some way to locate any hidden rooms. Maybe the Scarlet Rose did more than just block his magic. Maybe it was helping to keep him hidden. But at least he knew his mother was still looking for him.

As he was sitting there thinking about his mother his captor entered. Only they weren't alone this time. There were two of them wearing the same cloak and the same mask. They stood facing him and then took off their masks.

There were two women facing him. One of them looked familiar. He was sure he had seen a picture of her in the books his mother had written about her travels in other realms. He was pretty sure she was Richard's mother. The other looked familiar as well but he couldn't place her. Both women were rather old.

They told him his time in captivity would be coming to a not very pleasant ending if he didn't tell them everything they wanted to know about Wonderland and especially about his mother. They had been listening to his conversations with Alice long enough to know he was a very clever boy. He had figured out they were listening and had been careful about what he said.

They sat down on the bed and started asking him questions. At first he refused to answer but then they started making threats to his family. They told him that they already killed the First Elf and they would kill everyone he loved if he didn't give them what they wanted. He didn't know that killing the First Elf had been an accident. They hadn't realized that the defensive spell they had been given would merge with his magic when he was wearing the Scarlet Rose. Because they were touching him when they let the spell loose it had amplified. They didn't have any magic of their own.

Nicholas began to answer their questions with lies. However, he used just enough truth to make his lies believable. When they asked him about secret passages into the castle he told them where they were but omitted the fact that there were guards just inside each one as well as stationed along the length of them at odd intervals. He told them about most of the staff in the castle but left out the ones who could do magic. He told them where the private library of Scarlet's was but neglected to mention that she kept all her books about magic in a secret room only she could access.

He outright lied to them about the Wonderland Tree and the fact that it was a sentient being. He told them that it was born of magic and could be changed by magic but no more. He didn't tell them that if the tree died then Wonderland would die with it.

They spent hours asking him questions and writing down his answers. They sometimes repeated questions in different ways to see if he changed his answers but he had an excellent memory. After a few hours they woke Alice in her mirror and asked her to verify that he was telling the truth. She pretended to be outraged that he would betray Wonderland like that. She even broke into tears as she confirmed everything he said was true.

The women seemed delighted with all of the information. They sat going over everything and making plans as if they were alone. Nicholas pretended to be miserable as he listened to them while inside he was thinking that they couldn't win if they used what he gave them.

After they left, Alice looked like she wanted to say something. He tried to convey to her with his eyes to be careful; that they were probably still watching to see if they would reveal it was all lies. She opened and closed her mouth several times before starting a tirade about his betrayal of everyone. She ended by turning her back and refusing to speak to him. He laid down on the bed and pretended to cry into a pillow.

The next day the old women returned to the room but they weren't alone. They had a young man with them. He said a few words and Alice was released from the mirror. A few more words and both he and Alice were bound by magic ropes. He then opened a portal and they all stepped through into Wonderland.

Chapter Forty Five

It was the day of the week that Scarlet hated most. The day she met with people from throughout Wonderland in order to hear their concerns. She had kept this going because as the Queen she needed to put the needs of her realm above her own misery.

The search for Nicholas continued but it was like he had vanished into thin air. Even her suspicions about the two old Queens had amounted to nothing. Sure, she had thought they were lying but she had never been able to prove anything.

She was down to the last person to meet with when they were interrupted by a clamor outside the doors. Scarlet jumped up to go see what was going on when the doors opened and Nicholas came running toward her. His movements were awkward because he was still bound by the magic rope.

Right behind him the guards dragged in the two old Queens and Alice. Scarlet's face showed her hurt at the sight of Alice with them until Nicholas spoke up. He told Scarlet that Alice had been their prisoner as well and of all the help she had been to him. Scarlet removed their magical ropes and in one flick of her wrist had them tied around the Queens. Alice rushed forward to embrace her friend.

Nicholas warned Scarlet about the young magician who had been with them who had escaped. The Queens had tried to sneak them in through one of the secret passages he had told them about. They were halfway down it when they were ambushed by guards and dragged to the throne room so Scarlet could see them. The magician had somehow managed to melt into the wall and escape.

Nicholas and Alice told Scarlet everything that had happened from the time Alice was kidnapped. Scarlet tried to remove the Scarlet Rose from around

Nicholas' neck but she wasn't able to. This was some kind of powerful magic. She didn't know anyone who would be able to do it now that the First Elf was gone.

Regina and Theo both tried to remove it as well with no luck. Then all three of them tried together with no success. The two Queens watched it all with glee. Finally Scarlet turned on them to ask their reasoning. She really wasn't surprised when they said they wanted revenge for the way she had ruined their lives. She understood the one who had wanted to control others but she didn't understand the vain one.

Technically she was still the Queen in her realm. She still had a say in the way things were run. According to Dean she had become quite the political mind since her husband's death. She didn't understand what was going on until she noticed that the vain Queen referred to the control Queen for everything. She thought that maybe the control Queen had found a way to control her.

Scarlet sent out a search party to try to find the young magician. The Queens wouldn't tell her anything about his part in their plot.

Before the search party could return the land was rocked by an earthquake. Before they could even move people came running into the throne room to tell them the Wonderland Tree was burning.

Chapter Forty Six

Scarlet assigned some guards to stay behind and watch the two Queens. Then they all went running to the Wonderland Tree. The blaze was incredible to behold.

Nicholas could feel the tremors under his feet. He took in his surroundings as much as he could while running and saw that Wonderland was dying. When he saw that the blaze was killing his tree the tears began to pour down his face. He could hear the tree shrieking in agony.

The young magician was standing there and dousing the tree in magic fire. Nicholas didn't even think about what he was doing. He ran straight at the magician and tackled him to the ground. He stopped throwing flames at the tree as he fell. As Nicholas wrestled with the magician, Scarlet put out the flames.

Theo helped Nicholas finish restraining the magician before they all turned to survey the damage. The tree was trembling. Looking around they could see that Wonderland was still hurting.

They were all looking around at each other. No one seemed to know what to do. It was obvious the tree needed some kind of help.

Scarlet, Theo, and Regina tried to put their magic into it while speaking words of healing to it. It had worked before and they desperately hoped it would work again. After a while, though, they had to admit it wasn't doing any good. The ground was starting to shake harder.

Nicholas felt a burning sensation in his chest. He looked down and saw the Scarlet Rose was glowing. He could hear the tree whispering to him and knew what he had to do.

He walked forward with his arms outstretched. He walked right up and embraced the tree. As everyone watched he began to glow. Then he slowly started to meld with the tree. As he disappeared into the tree, the tree began to glow. Before their eyes it began to repair itself and the effects of that spread out into the land around it.

Scarlet fell to her knees with tears streaming down her cheeks. She had just gotten Nicholas back and now he was gone again. This time she didn't see how there was any hope of getting him back.

Scarlet reached out and placed her hand on the trunk of the tree and wept. She stayed there for hours before John finally put his arm around her and led her away.

Chapter Forty Seven

When Scarlet woke up she was alone. It took her a few minutes to remember what had happened. She felt the tears welling up as she pictured Nicholas in her mind. She saw him meld with the tree over and over again in her mind as the tears poured down her face.

She was surprised when she left the room and there was no one in the hallway watching over her. She went down to the throne room to see what everyone was doing and found it empty. She started wandering through the castle to see where everyone was.

She ended up down in the dungeon and facing the young magician where he sat in his cell. She stared at him through the bars. He seemed so familiar, yet she was sure she had never seen him before. He stood up and stepped closer to the bars. She gasped and took a step back.

It wasn't possible. Her eyes were playing tricks on her. Her grief must be messing with her mind. How else could Alex be standing there?

She had seen him die. She had been there for the burning ceremony where he was set adrift on the river and then magically lit on fire. He wasn't magic. This wasn't possible. There had to be some kind of explanation.

He watched her as she started at him. He could tell she was disturbed by his appearance. He offered to change it to something else if that would please her. He just thought they should be upfront about everything and that included his true identity.

That was when he launched into his explanation. Because of the deal he had made with Regina, he couldn't die. What the First Elf had done just killed his body. When they set fire to the body it released his spirit into nature. There had been a baby being born in Wonderland at that exact moment which was a huge stroke of luck for him; he didn't have to become a flower.

He had a double stroke of luck when the baby being born turned out to have magical ability. He hit the trifecta when he was able to take over the body and master it easily.

He had spent his entire life in this body up to this point studying magic; and more specifically Wonderland magic. She asked him if he was after revenge. He seemed a little confused by the question and assured her he had nothing to seek revenge for.

She asked him what he had been doing with the two Queens and why he had attacked the tree if not for revenge. His answer shocked her. He told her that he had just been doing what the tree had told him to do. She was sure she had misheard him. The tree?

He looked her directly in the eye and told her that the tree had planned it all out from the beginning. The tree had lured Nicholas from the castle that night. The tree had planned the kidnapping. The tree has been running the show from the very beginning. Scarlet couldn't understand why.

Apparently the tree has been siphoning magic from Nicholas for years. The tree knew that if Nicholas felt that Wonderland was in trouble he would give his power to the tree. Now that the tree had all of Nicholas' magic it had everything it needed. Even as they spoke, the tree was becoming human.

Chapter Forty Eight

Scarlet turned and ran. She ran all the way from the castle to where the Wonderland tree stood. She pushed her way through the crowd that was surrounding the tree to see it with her own eyes. Standing in the middle of the crowd where the Wonderland Tree had been, there stood a man.

He was an old man with long white hair and a long white beard. He was bent over a cane. He actually resembled a gnarled old tree. Scarlet wasn't fooled by his appearance, though. She could feel the power radiating off him.

She pushed the rest of the way through the crowd until she was standing face to face with him. She didn't know what she had planned to do but she knew she had to do something. He reached out and took hold of her arm and the next thing she knew they were standing in the throne room alone.

He held up his cane and two chairs appeared in front of her. He indicated that she should sit in one of them while he sat in the other.

He took her hand in his and watched her face as he spoke. He told her that everything had been set in motion the day she brought the Estrella back into Wonderland. Having the magic back in the realm had woken him up. He had spent too long as a tree. He wanted to be human again. See, he was the magician whose magic had created Wonderland.

The Estrella had been his life force. He had created the Estrella and sent it through a portal because his body was dying and he wasn't ready for that. He hadn't anticipated the portal turning him into a tree or the magic being sucked out of him as it created the new land.

He had felt the pull of the True Love Tree when it bloomed. He had been so sure that amount of magic would restore him. All of the magic used to heal him after the lightning strike had given him just enough power to get to the True Love tree. He had melded with it with the surety that it would make him human again.

He had been so disappointed when it hadn't worked. He had found the answer when Nicholas was born beneath his canopy. Nicholas was born of the same true love that had created the True Love tree. If Nicholas would meld his magic with the tree then his humanity would restore the old magician to human form.

Scarlet asked him how he could possibly do this to her. She had healed him over and over again. If he had really been that desperate to be human again she would have helped him. Did he really have to take her son from her?

He explained to her that her son's magic had combined with the magic from the True Love tree because they were the same. The combination was what had made it possible. It wouldn't have worked any other way. He told her he was sorry for her loss but it was necessary. If he had stayed connected to Wonderland in that way everyone would die.

She just stared at him. He could see the incomprehension on her face. He told her that his magic was dying. If he was still rooted to the land when that happened then all of Wonderland would die. Becoming human stopped that from happening. Now they faced a bigger problem.

Wonderland had to have some kind of magic directly connected to the land in order to survive. There had to be a new tree. He had just enough magic left in him to help her create a new one. The problem was, it was going to take all of her magic to do it.

Chapter Forty Nine

They set to work immediately. They worked together to create a new amulet. She channeled every ounce of magic she had into it. They took it out to where the tree had stood. They planted it and waited.

And nothing happened. The new tree should have begun to grow immediately. John found them as they were trying to figure out what went wrong. John listened to their explanation. He suggested that maybe the sacrifice needed to be bigger than just her magic.

They took hands and stared into each other's eyes. Without a word passing between them they made an agreement. Together they stepped into the circle right over where the amulet was buried. They embraced each other. The ground under them began to tremble. It seemed to rise up around them and join in their embrace. It rose higher and higher and when it finished they were melded together in the form of one big tree.

The old magician looked on with glee. This had worked out far better than he ever could have dreamed. He was free and now there was no left to stand in his way. The First Elf was dead. Regina was no match for him. He had the power of the True Love tree and Nicholas inside him. There would be no one to stop him now. Wonderland was his.

Part

Four

It all started with Alice. Now Alice was the only one left to save them all. She had no magic and no hope. But she had to try. Wonderland needed her.

Chapter Fifty

Regina's powers were stripped from her and she was locked away. The reborn Alex had his powers stripped away but he was set free. The rest of Wonderland was allowed to keep their magic but they were watched closely.

There was no happiness. The new Wonderland Tree was guarded carefully. It wasn't necessary for the survival of the land. The Old Magician knew that if anyone figured that out they would try to rescue Scarlet and John. He couldn't allow that to happen.

Nicholas was still alive inside him He was conscious of everything that was happening and was furious. He had no control and no way out.

It had been ten years since the old magician had taken over Wonderland. He called himself Seamus just so everyone had a way to refer to him that wasn't "Old Magician".

He had dealings with other realms None of them were on good terms because they had all been friends with Scarlet. They only dealt with him because he was so powerful. They were all afraid he would destroy their realms if they didn't.

He had Wonderland in his grip and every other realm was afraid of him. What more could he want?

Chapter Fifty One

He knew there was an underground resistance. He wasn't worried about it. He'd eliminated all the threats. There was no one left with enough magic to post a threat. They were too scared of him to try to unite their magic either. There was no guarantee they could beat him and they could end up powerless if they tried.

His problem with the resistance was that he was having no luck tracking them down. They hadn't made any moves against him. That was what really worried him. He couldn't squash them if he didn't know what they were doing.

So he hired Alice to help him flush them out. He knew her history. He had already given her back her Alex. Now he promised to give her back her magic if she would help him eradicate anyone who threatened him.

Alice wasn't turning up anything for him either. But this allowed him to keep an eye on her and Alex.

He went down to the dungeon to visit with Regina at least once a week. He knew all there was to know about Wonderland but he wanted to know more about where Regina came from. Her magic had restored Wonderland when it was dying from the theft of the Estrella. He had managed to strip her of magic but he couldn't tap into it to use it.

He had to make sure her magic was unique. That there wasn't someone else that could come from her original land with magic stronger than his. She shared her story and he believed her but she had been in Wonderland so long she couldn't remember where she came from. He couldn't travel there when he didn't know where there was.

He left from a visit to Alice and headed to the dungeon to meet with Regina. When he got there he found the guards sprawled on the floor and the door to her cell wide open. He tried to alert the remaining guards to look for her but they were all gone. He portalled over to Alice's place and found her cleaning up from their earlier visit while Alex was reading.

He wasn't sure if he should believe them or if they were in on it. They seemed genuinely shocked. They even jumped right in to help him with the search.

They searched for days but found no sign of anything. When the guards who were left behind woke up they couldn't remember anything. The next day they vanished as well.

Seamus was furious. Even without her magic Regina posed a threat. She could rally others to her side and amass an army to take him down.

Chapter Fifty Two

Regina had never really been stripped of her magic. That was why Seamus couldn't tap into it. Long ago the First Elf had moved her magic out of her body and into an enchanted object.

She stayed in the cell and let Seamus ask her his questions. She paid attention to everything he said and tried to figure out what his ultimate plans were. After ten years she gathered that they were really nothing more than what he had: rule Wonderland and strike fear into all other realms.

The guards were all loyal to Regina. Because Alice was working for Seamus she had access to the guards. She and Regina were able to converse back and forth through the guards.

Regina went underground when she left the cell. They agreed that Alice would stay where she was and continue working for Seamus. She would feed him just enough accurate information to keep him from getting suspicious. She would also keep track of him so that they could plan their moves carefully.

In the meantime, Regina was very quietly reaching out to allies in other realms. She was building a network of magic users to help her in the battle she knew would be coming.

She was also working on trying to remember where she had come from. She remembered having to hide her magic. She remembered the forced engagement and that being what made her flee. Her family would be long dead by this point. It was likely she wouldn't even be remembered there. But maybe she had a descendent there with the same kind of magic.

She had her friends in every realm searching through their archives for any mention of her. She really thought it was getting time for a family reunion.

It took several months but one of her allies finally found a record of her. The most amazing part was it was from the next realm over. She had had a younger brother when she fled. He had taken over ruling when her parents had passed on. The realm was still under the rule of that same family.

She worked it out with Alice that Alice would go to that realm to meet with the ruling family. Regina knew if she left Wonderland that Seamus would know. Alice was going to tell him that she had a lead on Regina's ancestry and was going to check it out. When she returned she would tell Seamus it had been a dead end.

She just really had to hope the trip took her a step closer to getting Wonderland out of Seamus' control.

Chapter Fifty Three

Alice cleared her trip with Seamus. She explained to him that one of her friends from the next realm over had found a book in their archives that appeared to be an old journal. It dated back to when Regina had first come to Wonderland.

Alice told him she wanted to look at the book herself rather than take her friend's word for it. She buttered him up by telling him that she was taking a page out of his book by not trusting anything she didn't see with her own eyes.

He let her go but insisted she take one of his people with her. She agreed and they left the next morning. When they arrived they were led to a private chamber and offered refreshments. Alice declined and asked to be taken to the book right away. Her companion insisted on needing something to drink.

He downed a glass of water quickly before reaching for a plate of cookies. His hand was still spread out in front of him when he fell asleep. Alice let out a little laugh as her host told her that he would sleep peacefully through the rest of the day.

She then led her out of the chamber and up to the library. They sat and discussed Regina's lineage. For a long time after Regina fled there was no magic in the land. Or if there was magic it was kept well hidden. It wasn't until Scarlet's urgent plea for help with the Wonderland Tree that the current King came forward and admitted he and his daughter both had magical abilities. His daughter had gone to Wonderland to study magic after that. Luckily she had finished her education and returned before Seamus took over.

The Princess wanted to return to Wonderland and help Regina take back the realm. Alice assured her they could use the help but wasn't sure how to get her into Wonderland. It was impossible to portal in and any magic user entering the borders instantly sent an alert to Seamus.

` The Princess, Skylar, told Alice that she had been studying far more than just the lore of the land. She had been studying topography. She had found a tunnel that led from the castle in her land to the outer woods of Wonderland. Alice got a huge smile on her face and told her that she had built that tunnel with magic long ago. She had forgotten all about it in the centuries since then.

She wasn't sure if Seamus' magical detection extended underground. If it did it could be fun to convince him his magic must be malfunctioning when all the mirror showed him was empty land with no one crossing over.

Alice and Skylar went back to the chamber where they left Alice's companion sleeping. He was still sound asleep with his arm reaching for a cookie. They set a half empty plate of dinner in front of him, then sat down themselves to eat. They were about halfway through their meal when he woke up.

The sleeping draught he had been given left him with a full memory of having spent the day in the library with the women pouring over old diaries and coming up empty handed. He woke up talking as if they were in the middle of a conversation and they just went along with it.

They headed back to Wonderland after they finished eating. Skylar was going to follow through the tunnel the next day with a small group of people who were determined to help Regina.

Chapter Fifty Four

Skylar arrived with no issues. Apparently the detection spell did not extend underground because the alarm didn't go off. Skylar and Regina immediately got to work.

They poured over magic books trying to find anything that would help. Skylar had two members of her party that she really trusted come into Wonderland above ground. They were going to try to get jobs in the castle so they could spy on everyone there.

The research was slow going and really not getting them anywhere. Skylar was actually going back and forth between Wonderland and her own castle. From there she was traveling around to other realms to recruit more help.

Regina felt good about their prospects. Skylar was incredibly smart and Regina was actually learning more about herself and her past. She didn't know how it would help anything but it was good to have the distraction.

Whenever she could, Skylar would bring back books from other realms. It was in one of these books that Regina finally found something that might help them overthrow Seamus.

There was a legend about a magic wand that could take the magic out of anyone unworthy. If they could track this wand down then their lack of magic wouldn't matter. The wand would put them on even ground.

Chapter Fifty Five

Seamus felt like he was going crazy. He couldn't tell who he could trust. If he didn't have Alice he didn't know what he would do.

She had become his most trusted advisor. She had managed to find several spies and arrest them for him. She had also given him some really good advice about which realms would make the best allies. This was why he was meeting with the Princess Skylar from the next realm over that day.

She had been helping Alice try to track down Regina's place of birth. Alice had made several trips to Skylar's realm. This time Skylar said she had something so exciting she wanted to deliver it in person.

She arrived with two very large books. The first was a very large history book from a very distant realm. The second was the key to translating the first.

Seamus knew he should delegate the reading of this book to someone else but other than Alice there was really no one he trusted. He had too much else for Alice to do so he took the reading upon himself.

Alice continued to come and go and do his errands for him. Princess Skylar was also turning into quite the ally. .She was very well connected and was able to put him in contact with people in other realms who could help him. He felt he was really building quite a following. He really felt that if it came to a war he would not be outnumbered.

Not that he really worried about that. There was no one out there with power equal to his. He may not be able to tap into what he took from Regina but had free use of what he took from Alex. And he was putting that to good use keeping the new Wonderland Tree guarded.

It still worried him that he didn't know what Regina was up to. But since she didn't have magic he didn't worry too much.

Chapter Fifty Six

After weeks of reading through every book she could find and having every ally she had searching, Regina finally found her answer. The magic wand had to be created; not found. The best part was that in tricking Scarlet into trapping herself in the form of a tree, he had given Regina the means necessary to create it. The tricky part would be getting near the tree to get what she needed.

The spell that Seamus was using to guard the tree meant he was the only one who could get near it. It was Alice who gave Regina the answer to this puzzle. She was certain that all Regina had to do was glamour herself to look like Seamus. Regina had never done glamour spells before so Alice worked with her; teaching her everything she knew about it.

Regina caught on quickly and within a few days was ready to try her luck. She glamoured herself to look like Seamus and then walked to where the tree was. She thought her glamour must be pretty good because they quickly hid when they saw her.

When she got to the tree she spoke quietly to it. She really hoped that Scarlet understood that it was her and not Seamus standing there. She explained the plan and what she needed from Scarlet. When she finished she stood and waited for any kind of sign that Scarlet understood her. She was just about to give up with the leaves began to rustle.

The tree bent toward her as if being blown by a strong wind. One of the branches began extending toward her as if it were growing. The branch broke off a smaller part of itself, about the size of Regina's arm, and laid it in her hand. Then it stood straight again as if it had never moved.

Regina hurried back to her hiding place so she could get to work. She would carve this branch until it looked like the wand in the pictures of the legend. There was a spell that needed to be carved into it and making the words that small was going to take a lot of concentration.

When she finally completed it, it was a thing of beauty. There was a large blue gem set into the top of it. The writing carved into it was done in a beautiful script. It was polished to a beautiful shine. Regina could feel the power of it just by being near it. When she held it in her hand she felt completely certain this would work.

She sent word through her network to all of her allies that they were ready. They would face Seamus in a week.

Chapter Fifty Seven

Seamus was so wrapped up in the book Skylar had given him that he didn't notice the travelers from other realms beginning to arrive. It wasn't until the magic detection spell started shrieking at him that he looked up.

Through the mirror he saw what basically looked like an army coming into Wonderland; there were so many people. He tried to summon Alice but she didn't come. He made his way out of the castle to find Alice and Princess Skylar standing with Regina. At first he thought they had captured her but then he quickly realized they weren't holding her there.

Every ally he thought he had was standing behind the three women and glaring daggers at him. He knew he could subdue the entire crowd with his magic. He let it build and flow down into his hands. He held them out in front of himself. Just as he released it at the crowd, Regina pulled out the wand.

Seamus not only felt the power being pulled out of him; he could see it. Everyone could see it. It flowed out of him and into the wand in bright rainbow lights.

When the light show stopped, Seamus fell to the ground. Everyone watched in shock as his body turned to dust. Regina seemed to be the only one who expected this. She turned to Alice and Skylar and explained that she thought this might happen. He was centuries old and his magic was the only thing holding him together.

Alice thought this was a far-fetched idea. She has been almost as old when she lost her magic. Regina told her she had thought of that. When Alice lost her magic it was because of dueling portals. Also, she hadn't been alone. Some of her magic went into Isabella. Seamus had nothing left to tie him to life. That was part of the spell inscribed into the wand. It locked away the magic it took.

Regina turned to address the crowd. She could see they were all a little wary of the power she held in her hand. She did her best to assure them that power would be used to keep Wonderland alive and nothing more.

Chapter Fifty Eight

Regina, Alice, and Skylar led the way as the crowd followed them to where the new Wonderland Tree stood. Regina walked up and placed her palm to the tree; then whispered a few words too low for anyone else to hear. She stepped back and held the tip of the wand to the trunk of the tree.

When she stepped back the tree looked like it was melting. When the melting stopped, Scarlet and John stood before them. Regina sank down to the ground and began to cry.

Once she had settled enough to be coherent, she stood to face her daughter. She explained her final theory about the wand and the power it held. She thought that because Nicholas had been bonded with Seamus they might be able to bring Nicholas back. She just didn't know how.

After months of research, though, they had no answers and Scarlet was slipping into a depression she wasn't sure she could get out of. She was holding the wand and thinking of Nicholas as she wept. A tear fell on the wand and the words of the spell lit up. The glow grew brighter and brighter.

Scarlet felt the wand begin to get warm in her hand. She set it down on the table and watched with fascination as it began to change shape. When it stopped glowing there was a baby laying on the table. She stepped forward to look closer and found she was looking at her Nicholas exactly as he was the day he was born; right down to the key birthmark.

She called out for everyone else to come quick. She had to make sure she wasn't seeing things. She had been so stressed and depressed about the whole thing that she couldn't be sure her eyes weren't playing tricks on her.

Everyone came running in and gasped over the baby. They had been expecting a return of the ten-year-old boy. Instead they got a chance to start over without the tree interfering. Things in Wonderland looked like they were going to be alright.

Epilogue

It all started with Alice. So much happened in Wonderland and Alice had been a big part of it all. Now here it was ten years after the reign of Seamus had ended. There were so many possibilities ahead for Alice and she reveled in all of it. She had Alex. She had friends. She had her students. She sat and talked with the flowers and together they pondered all the possibilities the future held.

The End

34543695R00172

Made in the USA
Middletown, DE
31 January 2019